I Beati Paoli
and the Devil's Hand

Charles S. Darwin III

ANDERSON, BERKLY AND STONE PUBLISHERS

Published and printed in the United States of America

The Beati Paoli and the Devil's Hand

Copyright 2011 Anderson, Berkley and Stone Publishers

To schedule speaking engagements, obtain special pricing for groups, or to learn more see

www.abspublishers.com   www.thebeatipaoliandthedevilshand.com

The Beati Paoli and the Devil's Hand/ Charles S. Darwin III – 1st ed.

ISBN-13: 978-0615587233

DEDICATION

To those who sacrifice self to relieve suffering in a community
asking nothing in return, they will achieve bodhicitta.

May it be so.

PREFACE

Scientists studying how hydrogen atoms form into helium; continue to contemplate helium forming even heavier more complex atoms. Eventually they see a beautiful pattern unfolding that illustrates the immutable laws comprising the foundational structure of nature. The first law reveals that no complexity can build without the help from something else: that is, it takes two of something <u>cooperating</u>, for a higher purpose other than self, to reach the next highest level of potential. The second law requires memory retention so that lessons can pass to future generations. The next is the ability to <u>communicate</u> needs and willingness to accommodate. Then there must be a common <u>goal</u>; and finally everything has to be <u>adaptable</u> to change. The most successful people on Earth know and honor these laws. I enjoy putting Stone Richards into situations where he feels compelled to remind himself and others who forget that life is not about self; nor is it about how much gold you can accumulate; life is about service to others, which allows us to achieve our highest potential together. The theme in all these stories is clear; humanity is stronger when everyone works towards common goals; and humans are still in their infancy compared to what their highest potential can be. I hope the possibilities offered in my books inspire you, as much as I enjoy presenting them. Modern philosophers talk about intent. Intent is well and good, but intent is nothing without action. Be inspired to contribute your verse: live with purpose, and convert your intent into action. Stand strong with your convictions, but remain open to knowledge. Evil is an ever-changing chameleon, but always with the same flaw of serving only a few at the sacrifice of the many. In the end, however, there is no I, we, or them; there is only one common destiny. A god does not predetermine what that destiny will ultimately look like, nor does some mystical prophet; the shape of humanities future, depends solely on choices made and the goals achieved by everyone working together. Either outcome, glorious or disastrous, will result from opposing forces cooperating, or not.

Charles S. Darwin III

TABLE OF CONTENT

IN ALL MATTERS WHATSOEVER

READ CRITICALLY

QUESTION EVERYTHING

GET INVOLVED

REMOVE MEDIOCRITY FROM YOUR LIFE

LIVE WITH PURPOSE

DIE WITH INTENT

Steven H. Lumbert
The Librarian: The Evolution of God and
Humanities Purpose

The Universe routinely offers gifts to random pedestrians. Accepting those gifts can be risky; especially when the goals of the universe are not completely understood. More times than not, the gifts are really tests offering an opportunity to awaken a life otherwise embroiled in mediocrity. Some gifts take the form of a dangerous challenge; or, a devastating disaster. No matter the outcome, the gift ultimately changes everything for the random pedestrian, and influences all of those exposed to the fallout. Gifts from the Universe mean to break symmetry, keeping the pot boiling and stirred.

1

THE UNIVERSE DELIVERS A CHALLENGE

After surviving a fierce storm at sea that lasted three days, Stone Richards awakens. He is now a cast-a-way, somewhere in the South Pacific Ocean, on a lushly vegetated and desolate volcanic island. Except for his boat, he is alone. *Spiritus* is on the rocks stranded offshore. Stone is well prepared to face his greatest test yet. Armed with the skills acquired during his military enlistment and the extensive scientific training obtained while studying at the University of Miami he is prepared to battle nature. These are his only survival tools; but for a few supplies and his Colt 45 magnum, all locked away on his marooned boat.

Just a few days had elapsed, since his convalescence began. During that period, he had explored less than a tenth of the small island. Along the volcano's steep and treacherous sides, he discovered that thermal vents were gushing out steam and toxic gases. Cracks and small crevasses surrounding the vents were rich with surface deposits containing rare minerals such as Uraninite; pitch-blende by another name; a primary source of Uranium 238, and other types of metals. Pitchblende refines into yellowcake and that fuels nuclear reactors, or bombs. In its natural form, uranium oxides are rarely lethal to humans.

Further, along his walks, mostly on level ground, Stone found trees with edible fruits: bananas, coconuts, and dates; and cacao the Incas once used to make energy drinks. Once again, the wind was returning to Stone's sails. With every passing day, he gained more confidence this test would be survived.

Then unexpectedly, another event challenged his existence on the Earth. An explosion, in the middle of the night, emanated from halfway up the mountain's side. The explosion illuminated the otherwise dark sky as though one were looking through a night scope. An ominous dust cloud formed, perhaps from the island's unique mixture of metals and minerals, combining with the extreme heat and pressures instantaneously created during the explosion. The cloud emitted a strange green luminescence seeming to last for hours before it finally floated out to sea. During that time, feeling like an eternity, everything was aglow, even Stone. The precise danger was unknown. The treat to his existence was clear.

Within hours, after the exposure to the green cloud, Stone began to vomit and have diarrhea that caused him to become dangerously dehydrated and weak. A fever began to build. After two days had past, Stone's hair began to fall out. His vomit and stool had become bloody. Those symptoms caused Stone to think he would soon begin to bleed out; he was sure the explosion exposed him to a lethal dose of radiation. Due to the immediate appearance of the symptoms of radiation sickness, Stone knew exposure to a dosage exceeding 8 to 10 Gy (Gray) occurred. A typical X-ray exposes patients to a dose well below 0.1 Gy. His brain was throbbing so hard, he feared it would escape the confines of the skull. With each beat of his pounding heart, his eardrums would stretch to their finite limits, drowning out all other sounds. That night, before he passed out from the pain and exhaustion, his last thoughts turned to how he might kill himself; not to avoid a tortuous slow death by a thousand needles, but to die on his own terms, not from a freak accident.

For the first time, Stone began to empathize with the dinosaurs he had mused over and studied for most of his professional life. They too endured a test when a game changing meteor struck the Earth, challenging every living thing that survived to quickly adapt or die.

Hours later, Stone, woke up from a deep comatose like sleep. It was the kind of deep sleep from which one awakes, when it takes a minute for the brain to reengage, and for the muscles to come alive. He was now abnormally hungry and thirsty, especially for someone with the symptoms of radiation poisoning. He found a few things to eat. His ravenous thirst was barely quenched with a few drops of water from a hot stagnate pool of water. For some strange reason he knew there was more water. Somewhere, he remembered there was a pool of cool clean sparkling water fed by a small waterfall. How did he know that? Where is it now, when he needed it most? It appeared he was losing his short-term memory.

Hurting from hunger and thirst, he slowly made his way to the ocean's edge looking for food. He was delirious. He warily moved about in a type of trance somewhere between awake and asleep. His clothes were tattered and smelt like rotting flesh. He was also barefoot. Shoes were the last thing on his mind. His head was still pounding but no longer aching. When he arrived at the shoreline, instead of finding shellfish, lobster, and a bounty of fish that would provide the protein he required, all he found were the floating, presumably poisoned, radioactive carcasses of dead fish lining the shoreline. Not one live fish existed. Stone fell to his knees in frustration and anguish. Once again, he started to feel the agonizing effects of hunger, thirst, and the excessive heat. Especially, he was experiencing the futility that follows.

All he could think of was eating. Just now, he could swallow anything that would fill the deep void felt in the pit of this stomach. He closed his exhausted eyes and thought of his favorite restaurant, Alfredo's Paradiso: more specifically, his thoughts turned to the fabulous seafood plates served there, filled with fresh shrimp, clams, and fish topped with a lemon butter sauce garnished with green olives, and capers. All dinners served with heavy, robust garlic bread made from whole grains and oats. There was always water, lots of clear cold water, and...

"Sassolino (Little Stone) my god! Are you-a ok? Where you come from?" asked the concerned proprietor, Alfredo. "You look-a mess; are you-a OK? Here, have some water. You look like a big cat been dragging you around."

There he was, in his white double-breasted jacket and a Toque: the typical apparel for a professional chef. His smile and warmth, as always, generously offered. Stone was still barefoot and in his tattered clothing, still smelly after what seemed days without bathing. Stone could only surmise he was dead.

He reached out to touch Alfredo, "Alfredo is that you?"

Alfredo had been making a pizza with his back to the bar. Normally, he could see anyone walking through the front door; if not, he could hear the bell ring when a customer opens the door. Alfredo did not see Stone walk in or hear the door open. This did not stop the concern he had for his apparently injured friend and patrono.

Alfredo and his wife Linda are first generation Italians from Sicily. Alfredo's father, Roberto, is a police officer with a vendetta against the mafia. Roberto spent much of his energy, hunting them down to face justice. Even now, many years later, it is a dangerous time for the entire family. The Mafia is an exclusive club that has a very long memory that reaches across every ocean. Family members are never out of bounds when retaliation is the goal.

Alfredo abhorred violence of any kind, he is more an amante della vita (a lover of life). He finds beauty in simple things and works hard to support his family. He is a pragmatic person. There are no dreams for Alfredo; there is only hard work and rein-vestment when opportunity aligns with established objectives. After marrying Linda, his childhood sweetheart from Sicily, both moved to New York City to blaze their own trail through the forest of American Dreams. He had heard so much about the land of promise and opportunity, and felt it would shield his new family from the pain and corruption that is so much a part of every Sicilian's urban life.

There are people who are born who cannot escape their destiny: no matter how hard they try. Even if they run away from the things they hate most, like violence; destiny makes them play the game—voluntarily, or not.

Stone realized long ago that everything in the Universe is entangled. That means nothing happens that does not influence something else—nothing. For instance, when a butterfly flaps its wings in Africa, it begins a series of micro events that can ultimately generate a devastating hurricane destined for a place like a coastal community along the United States. Ultimately, the hurricane destroys billions of dollars worth of property. As a result, many people suffer losses on the one hand; on the other, one man about to lose his family's home, because he had been out of work for three years, finally gets a job that puts his family back on a stable financial track. Everything is entangled-everything.

That one simple routine decision, made by Linda and Alfredo, moving to America, ultimately affected the lives of an entire nation. The result of that decision awoke legends of *I Beati Paoli*, a clandestine group of honorable men that ruled the Sicilian countryside for hundreds of years. The awaking of that legend called upon a devil to bring their legacy and purpose for living back to life. This time there would be no legend, it was very real. Some unfortunate enough to fall into its tang-led web called it **Las mano del Diavolo**; others called it, The Devil's Hand.

Alfredo's first restaurant was in New York City in Times Square, *Alfredo's New York Style Pizzeria.* Nevertheless, after a short honeymoon with the city and its people, they had to leave. Just like in Sicily, the mafia began to invade their livelihoods, using threats and intimidation. The cities' slim would force unfair 'taxes' onto business owners for picking-up their garbage, or for the protection from other crooks, who set spontaneous fires. The Slim had sticky tentacles that reached high into the city's most vulnerable infrastructure, and deep into the elected official's pockets.

One morning just before opening the front doors, three goons entered Alfredo's Pizzeria from the back alley. After slapping him around a few times to get his attention, the Mafioso grabbed the stunned proprietor dragging him into the bathroom. As one goon held Alfredo's head under the dirty toilet water, another poured tomato sauce into the mix.

"So Bobbie, what you think this idiot was thinking, he gonna not pay us the pizzo and let his garbage continue to build-up in the back? That's a health hazard. Someone could die of a horrible disease.

"Hey Alfie, you can hear me with all that shit and sauce in your ears? Don't squirm you capra amante malato (sick goat lover), you gonna get shit and sauce all over my new shoes. You think the cities gonna come get your garbage? They don't do that anymore, we do. And when you don't pay, we can't feed our children. You want our children to die, you selfish dirt-bag?

"We gonna be back tomorrow and you better have the full payment plus interest for late charges. For now, we gonna take a down payment from the cash register. You have a good day, OK? Bobby, Marco takes him out back and shows him how big a mesh needs to be cleaned up out there."

After kicking and beating Alfredo some more, Bobby and Marco threw him unconscious next to the dumpster. As a final affront, they tore open black plastic bags of rotting food, and then dumped it on him.

Violence and intimidation was nothing new to Alfredo, he had seen those many times before in Sicily. It is what bullies do. Violence is the spawn of ignorance. It cripples a bully's drive to do anything else, and tattoos them with the moniker of slim. Slim that is very similar to sticky wet waste products, like those left behind by slugs and snails. Nonetheless, because nothing is worthless, because everything is entangled, even slim serves a purpose, this time it is to awaken the legends of history.

Marco said to Alfredo, before leaving with Bobby, "Like Vinnie said, 'It ain't healthy back here, someone gonna die of a horrible disease if it ain't cleaned up.' See you in the morning shit-sauce. Be sure to wash your hands before going back to work. That's another health rule, byes-the-way."

A few moments later, it was a stranger that walked out of the shadows to help Alfredo get to his feet. The Stranger helped lead the wounded and bruised Alfredo into the bathroom, so he could clean-up. The Stranger walked to the phone behind the counter calling for an ambulance. Afterward, he walked back to the bathroom, bringing with him some towels and soap for Alfredo.

Alfredo was spitting up blood. The Stranger was concerned that Alfredo might have internal injuries. The Stranger's hand moved into Alfredo's body. Still dazed and hurting, Alfredo was unaware that what some would call a miracle was happening. The Stranger did not believe in miracles, everything had an explanation. It was not beyond him, however, to use the ignorance and superstition of fools to dispel the evil that it spawned. "Don't move around for a few minutes my friend, rest. Think of those things that make you happy. This is just one event of many more. We make our world, as we want it to be. Imagine the one that makes your life happy. Breathe slowly."

The Stranger's hand moved about feeling the organs inside of Alfredo's bludgeoned torso. It was on the stomach that the Stranger felt fluids pumping out into the surrounding cavity. His fingers formed a clamp around a small tear, stopping more fluids from pouring out. "Remain calm my friend: breathe slowly." After a few minutes, the Stranger removed his fingers. The fluids had stopped flowing. It was a small wound.

"I am sorry my friend I could not help sooner. There are reasons unexplainable at this moment: perhaps for a greater purpose, one person must suffer alone the selfishness of fools. There are no rewards or vengeance today: Perhaps tomorrow: so until tomorrow my friend. Take comfort in knowing that in your future there is success, warm weather, and sunshine waiting for you in Florida."

The paramedics arrived. The Stranger told them Alfredo was beat up and that he was spitting up blood. There is a wound on his front stomach lining near the left side. One paramedic looked at him as if he had three noses, and then asked, "You got an X-ray machine in your briefcase, or you just stealing sausages? The other asked, "You a doctor, Mack? If not, get the hell away from us, and let us do our jobs."

"Remember, front stomach lining, left side, a small wound."

"Yea, yea got it, small stomach wound."

The next moment the Stranger was gone. Alfredo was too hurt and sick to his stomach to ask the Stranger's name or even to look him in the face. He never learned who the Stranger was.

It wasn't long after that brutal morning, Linda and Alfredo closed the restaurant leaving New York for good. They eventually found a new home in Merritt Island, Florida. It was as far away from illegal crooks as they could get. To their chagrin, however, they soon found that legitimate crooks had replaced the illegal ones. Petty bureaucrats would come into their establishment finding ridiculous issues for which they could collect big fines that justified their employment. These agents of the government also had to make a living. At least that was how Alfredo justified paying the ludicrous fines. At least they do not break legs, he would say; and they only come every few months instead of every week. It still cost him less, this legalized pizzo: this extortion money.

"What do you be thinking? Of course it's-a-me. Sassolino you been making too much limoncello again and not sharing it with you friends?" asked Alfredo. "Nice-a haircut. Looks-a real cheap to maintain." Stone was unaware he had become completely bald from his exposure to the radiation.

Stone stood up from the bar stool without answering and wandered over to the front door. He opened it and walked outside, looking north towards the Target shopping mall. He could smell the hot asphalt from the Merritt Island parking lot invade his senses. Engineers and developers in this area had an imagination about the size of a flea's ass when it came to building sustainably. Nonetheless, it seemed real to be standing near his home in a jungle of concrete and asphalt, built with absolutely no forethought of the future. To the developer there was no legacy, only the profit for this day. Perhaps this was a very vivid dream. He read once that during a near death experience, dreams could seem very real. At least it was a good dream: there was water, food, and air conditioning: if you are going to die, at least die sated.

"Sassolino," called Alfredo, "Come, you get-a in here, out of the heat. You look kind-a sick. Come in now, please, before you fall down and sue the socks off my feet. Sit down. Drink some water, you want-a something to eat? Let me make you something real fast."

Stone turned, still dazed by what he was experiencing; he walked back into the restaurant and sat down. Alfredo filled a metal pitcher with ice and water; afterward, putting that and a cold glass of ice water on top of the bar. Stone picked up the pitcher without thinking, drinking it down until empty. Then he drank the glass of water. "Alfredo, I can sit in the kitchen, I am not dressed to sit here."

"Of course, you are a mess, you must have worked hard today. Sit at your bar seat, downwind per favore. What you got in your pockets anyways? Regardless, I say if you cannot be-a proud of your friends in their worst-a moments, are you really a friend at their best? What does my friend want to eat?"

After eating and drinking his fill, Stone laid his exhausted head down on the cool bar top and fell fast asleep. Alfredo had moved the empty plate just in the nick-of-time. When Stone eventually woke-up it was morning, but now he was on top of the covers of his ruffled bed. His feet were still bare, and he was still in his rancid and tattered clothing. The phone began to ring; Stone answered it, "Hello?"

"Sassolino, where you be? You disappeared yesterday without a word. Are you ok?

Stone was slowly looking around trying to figure out where he was now, trying to understand what was going on; was he still on the beach? Was he still breathing? Was he dead? What is that smell? Can the dead really smell themselves? Where is the beach? Where is the *Spiritus*?

"Alfredo, I don't know if I am ok or not. The last thing I remember I was ship wrecked on an island in the south pacific, and then I survived some sort of explosion. The explosion seemed to have exposed me to a lethal dose of radiation. I needed food and water and I ended up at your place. Now I find myself in my bed, I have no idea how I got here."

"The last thing you should remember, you son-of-a-beach is that you walked out on your tab. Now what is going on? Do you want me to come get you to the medico (doctor)? You sound-a crazy: more so-a, perhaps, than normal."

"Let me call you back Alfredo, I will stop by later today."

"Ok, Sassolino, but you lay off that limoncello, ok? Bring it here, I will take it from you. You have too much. Ok?

"Ok, my friend."

Stone hung-up the phone, and began to walk around the room: He looked out the windows, then opened and closed the doors: he rubbed his face hard with both his hands. He still did not notice his missing beard. It looked as if he was home, at least in his dream he was. Every bone in his body, every muscle, was aching and that never happened in a dream before: adding to that his mouth and throat were dry. He still had an unquenchable thirst. He walked into the bathroom, stripped down, and entered the shower.

"I still must be dreaming. I am passed out on the beach," Stone was talking to himself. "But then again the water feels so real, it is cold and soothing." He further realized that his energy was returning. The shower was invigorating. It seemed like every cell in his body was taking a drink and then instantly relaxing. The soap-suds turned into a thick lather. After scrubbing off the dead skin cells, oil, and dirt, his skin began to squeak so loud, it could make an Imam giggle.

At one point, his hand moved to the pubic area, it was slick and smooth as a babies butt, there was no hair. His scalp was also slick; he had become completely bald. "Where in the blazes is my beard? What the hell?" Stone was again talking aloud to himself.

He vividly remembered an explosion and the beginning of his hair loss. That was when he realized he had been exposed to some sort of radiation originating from the explosion on the island. Was he still on the island in a coma? Alternatively, was he here in his house? If he is home in a dream, where is his hair? He would never dream of being shaven. Stone has had a beard and long hair since the day he walked out of the gates at Cannon Air Force base with his honorable discharge. That was when he started his new life as a civilian; far away from all the deceit and death, he survived over seven years while fighting clandestine battles. During that time, he was an intelligence field officer, working undercover as an engineer. He quietly carried with him, some of his countries darkest secrets that he never exposed—missions he would never forget. His beard was as much a part of him as his arms or legs; it was the opposite of what the military tried to make him. He would never dream of shaving it off. Nonetheless, it was gone. Furthermore, this moment did not feel like a dream to Stone.

Even after the shower, however, he was still tired and hungry: dead tired. Stone walked to his closet and opened the doors. He selected a pair of new khaki pants, a khaki shirt, and adorned his sun burnt feet with new leather sandals. He then walked over to the end of the bed and sat down. He fell backwards onto the bed. Once again, he dropped off into a deep sleep—refreshed but still exhausted.

When the Universe calls upon you to perform a task, it leaves no instructions. That is the test. The Universe never micro-manages. It is up to you to survive the test, or die trying. If you survive the first trial there will be another waiting, and then another; this will continue until your time is up, and you finally die.

2

THE CALLING

Waves, vicious huge waves the size of skyscrapers are crashing down and crushing the *Spiritus* along with her weary, wet, and tired Captain. He had been fighting this storm for three days without sleep. Stone was exhausted.

A harness tethered him to the boat. That way his body would not wash over if he passed out. The sky was black. There were no stars anywhere to help orient the Captain. He could not see more than a few feet in front of him.

This was an off-season storm no one predicted or saw coming. It formed very quickly over the abnormally hot Pacific Ocean waters. It was another product of global warming and sea level rise. Stone was getting punch-drunk from a lack of sleep. He was thinking someone could get an eye poked out if not careful. It would have been nice if there was a 'they or someone', but Stone foolishly decided to single hand his boat to Tahiti.

Worse than being at sea alone in the night, during a raging storm, is being present in that space of time lying between waves a hundred feet high. There one can only wait in horror for the next unseen wave to come smashing down, drowning everything with ice-cold seawater, while abruptly overturning the only dry platform in the middle of an enormous angry ocean.

As the seas build under the boat, one begins to rise rapidly, like being in an elevator. As the boat tosses and turns, all one can do is keep hanging on, then take a breath as the sea consumes your little world. The boat begins to tumble, and then uncontrollably, it slides down the side of the mountainous wave.

It was for the lack of anything else to do, the boat being tossed about like a tiny cork, Stone would begin counting while the boat was positioned upside-down with the mast and sails underwater; anticipating with his breath held, the moment when the boat would right itself and once again give him a dry place to stand and breath. His personal best was two minutes underwater without swallowing a drop. It took every ounce of energy he had to endure the painful timeframes between the building of the first wave, and the crashing down of the next.

The first thing Stone learned as a geological oceanographer, never screw around with the ocean. It was too easy to become a punching bag, slapped around by the biggest force known to humanity. Stone kept thinking that the ocean was pissed at someone or something, and meant to get its point across. Stone was obviously in a fierce melee between forces of nature unleashing and mixing their pent up energies. These forces of nature were intent on changing landscapes. He was definitely in the wrong place, at the wrong time.

Then again, there are no accidents. He was in the middle of this storm for some reason--besides his stupidity. For some other reason he has survived. He should have died a hundred times before, over the last 72 hours.

Never abandon your boat—never! That is an immutable law of the sea. If you are not stepping up into your life raft, you are messing up. Boats adrift at sea are discovered everyday with their sails in the water and the hatches fully open. Even after months or years of enduring storms and heavy seas, boats remain intact, even without a crew. The boats left to drift about because their captains and crew prematurely abandoned them, voluntarily or perhaps not. Sailboats easily endure the punishments of the sea; humans do not. When the seas got so bad, it became impossible to control the boat, ancient sailors would take the sails down, seal the hatches, and then find a place in the cabin to tie each other in place; the boat left at the mercy of the storm. In the end, however, if it was well constructed, the boat and the crew survived. Never leave your boat. That is unless nature throws you off to fend for yourself.

Thousands of miles from civilization, these were the final moments before the hull of the *Spiritus* collided with the uncharted rocks in the middle of the Pacific Ocean. The only sounds heard were the sickening cracks and pops of dreams and inspirations, destroyed as fiberglass meets rock, in the middle of a pitch-black storm filled night. Stone's head was spinning as his only life support continued to twist and roll on the rocks, made worse by the massive waves crashing down from all directions.

During these final moments, the last thing Stone remembered, after his tether snapped apart, was the ice-cold Pacific water washing over him then violently jerking him up and off the deck. His body dragged across jagged surfaces moments before total darkness overcame his fear.

It was either the morning sunlight, or perhaps the distant rainbows that woke him up from a slight concussion. In either case, after slowly prying his salt encrusted eyes opened, a white beach, comprised of little round pebbles, came into focus. Small waves continued to lap over his legs still submerged in the clear, green, and now calm water. He had survived another test. Still, there was no time for resting; the remaining energy in his body had to be used to find desperately needed water, then protein. Surviving the storm merely signaled the start of the next race. Life does not offer time-outs; death provides those.

Before daring to move, Stone took stock of possible injuries, while filling his lungs with the sweet smell of land that permeated the cool morning air. Pushing himself up onto his knees, he could see a tall lushly vegetated mountain: it was over eight thousand feet high. Clouds were hiding the summit. Closer was a dune line, vegetated with coconut palms, banana trees, and bamboo.

A troop of giant coconut crabs (*Birgus latro*) were standing close-by looking like multi-armed vultures smacking their hairy little beaks: apparently, waiting to begin their snack immediately after the stinking flesh in front of them stopped moving about. Protein is a rare treat for these island creatures that can grow to over 4.1 kilos (9 pounds). Years ago when her missing plane surfaced, some suspected these monsters ate Amelia Earhart's remains, her bones carried down and hoarded into their deep burrows.

Stone did not intend to be eaten alive, so he stood up: the monsters began to move away to his relief; he had no energy for an early morning crab-wrestling match that would surely end in someone's death. Just then, his stomach began to growl a bit, his thoughts turned immediately to the idea of roasting their tasty white flesh over a fire and mixing it with coconut meat and the residual coconut juices, along with a few bananas. No matter how endangered this animal was, if it came down to survival, it was their fault they did not evolve enough mobility to move off this small island. Anyway, who had ever heard of a crab that would drown if submerged in water for more than an hour? The ugly things deserved to be on a menu; if for no other reason than their lack of ingenuity. Perhaps even to avenge Amelia's remains. In any case, a proper excuse will surface should the Deserted Pacific Island Wildlife Police stop by.

It might have been due to the size he had grown to as he stood up, from their perspective, Stone had grown to become a giant! The little monsters decided it was time to retreat and began to scurry-away back to the safety of the trees and the vegetation line.

Before Stone could feast on protein, the first thing he needed was water. This was the most rapacious thirst he had ever experienced in his life. He knew if he did not find water soon, he would pass out or be dead in a matter of hours. He felt the symptoms of heat stroke beginning to set in: cold sweats, unset stomach, and headaches plus dizziness and weakness: all swirling around and coming at him from different directions, while he fought-off the desire to give-up and just black out.

Stone turned to look behind him. There, less than a thousand feet away, was the *Spiritus* high above the water: thankfully, but still hard on the rocks. The bad thing about fiberglass is that it is very brittle, especially when engaging coral reefs and rock outcrops. The good news is, if by some miracle, the boat survives a rocky engagement with only a few holes, repairs are easily cobbled together with the need of only a few resources, and some primitive tools.

Spiritus was apparently as hard to kill as her captain was. For years, both have been on a never-ending adventure. They have endured both metaphorical and very real storms frequently causing both to smash into rocks; both survived these harrowing encounters with man and nature put in front of them by serendipity. Afterwards, Stone always seemed more optimistic about life than he had been before, knowing instinctively, and from experience that rainbows always await voyagers when they emerge from the blackness of storms.

Spiritus sings to Stone as breezes blow through her rigging. Timeless messages past and present translated for Stone offered as inspirations whispered during quite moments. Inspirations that give Stone ideas that can serve others, helping them to obtain a more joyful life showing them how to live sustainably within the boundaries of their limited resources.

It seemed that just months before, he and *Spiritus* were in Haiti helping the earthquake victims build farm cooperatives, with the help of Hollywood's biggest A-list celebrities. On those farms, people could live and work for the cost equivalent of harvesting just 9 Tomatoes a Day. The reality show that helped to build the first farm is still taping in other project areas; any actor or would be actor is fighting for a break to get on the show. Some actors from the first show have returned to keep helping where they can.

It was a mistake to think of these people as do-gooders. Building farms that alleviate poverty are in every person's interest. Spending one dollar solves multiple problems that plagued global economies and livelihoods. The *9 Tomatoes a Day* program is a profitable business plan, cloaked in altruism.

After Haiti, Stone inadvertently sailed *Spiritus*, with his other love Janet, to the Niger Delta. Upon sailing into the worst undisclosed oil spill the world had ever seen, he helped to devise a plan to clean up the delta: additionally, he encouraged terrorists to become community leaders and environmental advocates, instead of targets for bullets and bombs delivered by profiteers. As a result, small villages became economic hubs of innovation and more so, eco-tourist destinations, because of the unique natural beauty and the new found joy for living the natives discovered.

There was another reality program after the one in Haiti, but only battlefield tested camera people could work on that programming. There had been too many targets of opportunity for misguided profiteers, disguised as terrorists, to blow up, or otherwise destroy. In the end, even in that mess, the ideas of helping the least among us rose above the forces that propagate poverty: ideas came alive that help empower people so they can control their daily lives: vision and hope defeated hate, corruption, and prejudice.

Even before all those adventures, during his first assignment in the military, stationed in Crete, Stone uncovered and stopped a gun for drugs network in the Middle East sponsored by renegades in the American government. He discovered that those deals were funded by counterfeit dollars. That operation, if unchecked, threatened to throw the entire global economy into a free fall.

Stone's team was now gearing up to serve the war torn region of the Democratic Republic of the Congo where children were kidnapped, brain washed, and turned into reluctant soldiers. Some are being forced to kill and rape indiscriminately, forced to support bands of rebels (gangsters by any other definition), whose only goal was to get rich by controlling the country's vast wealth of natural resources. This is where gold, diamonds, and cobalt, zinc, copper, and aluminum, and of course oil, quenched greedy appetites. A war of ideologies like religion, politics, and national pride, or humanities common goal had no place in the Congo: it was all about greed. This is where the worst genocide since World War II occurred that killed 5 million people between 1998 and 2003. The killing continues with over 500,000 people dying each year. This is where the psychopathic King of Belgium, Leopold II murdered fifteen million Congolese so he could corner the natural rubber market. This will be the next battleground for humanities sake. This project will test the limits of the edicts proposed by the 9 Tomatoes a Day farm program.

The Congo weighed heavily on Stone's mind for the last few months. Many governments, and wealthy families living in the darkness that dwells behind the shadows, depend on the ill-gotten gains that end with the senseless killing of the Congolese people. An example of this senseless violence was the assassination of the democratically elected leader, Prime Minister Patrice Lamumba, by the Belgium and American government, to ensure the uninterrupted flow of minerals and wealth. If the greedy dared call, visionaries like Lamumba a communist, as an excuse to murder him: Stone would not be immune. Stone needed more help than he had ever mustered before to survive the Congo Conspiracy.

Stone had left the Niger Delta just after meeting with the Eastern Congo Initiative where discussions took place to form an alliance that would build farm cooperatives in that country.

At the same time, John Prendergast from the Enough Project and a partner of the Eastern Congo Initiative was heading to a Congressional hearing in Washington, DC to push for the appointment of a special US Envoy to the Congo. A person with enough political influence needed to force movement out of the State Department. There was important legislation--the Conflict Minerals Act--that encouraged American companies to disclose where their raw materials came from. That way socially attuned consumers could choose to buy only from those companies that purchased minerals and other raw materials from countries whose leadership **do not** enslave, kill, and rape villagers that are in the way of mineral resources.

The crooks in the Congo use the minerals to feed their delusions of power and greed, instead of using the State's resources to build infrastructure like schools, hospitals, and roads, and factories. John is an activist that insists it is the purchase of these natural resources that keep the military, the rebels, and the corruption in all governments actively involved; while hundreds of thousands of innocent people die, waiting for the world to realize how their participation causes the pain to continue.

John also advocates the arrest or elimination of the top military leaders and government officials that commit crimes against humanity. Criminals must realize they cannot do harm with impunity. Some call it the Bin Laden protocols, two shots and a splash.

Even though it seemed like just a few months, many more have passed-by since the first 9 Tomatoes a Day program began: indeed it had been many long years of grueling difficult encounters with dangerous opponents that despised what Stone was doing. His work empowered the poor, and that took power away from the rich. The poor's poverty was the source of cheap labor and the reason the armed, the powerful, and the corrupt were able to plunder a country's natural resources for their own benefit, not that of the nation. Everywhere Stone encountered poverty and conflict, the root cause was always the abuse of, and demand for the natural resources. The 9 Tomatoes a Day program changed all that where it took root. Amazingly, somehow, Stone had stayed just one-step ahead of the bullets.

After the Niger Delta, Stone wanted to do something for his self and for Janet. He had read the writing on the wall, instinctively knowing that his work had recently pissed off profiteers reaching into the highest levels of the World's economy. If he wanted to continue making progress, lifting people out of poverty, it would take much more than his Colt 45 magnum and his tenacity. He would need the help of an international intelligence force dedicated to the same cause; which seemed unlikely, because the profiteers controlled most of the intelligence agencies; or at least he would need the help from a greater power, which also seemed unlikely.

Nonetheless, he wanted, or rather, he needed a breather to revitalize his thoughts and energy. He did so by getting close to nature. Within natures cradle, he contemplates humanities place in the Universe and the possibilities they could enjoy once their highest potential begins to spring forth. From evolutions perspective, humans are still infants playing in a sand box.

Stone had never before seen a live duck-billed platypus (*Ornithorhynchus anatinus*), a funny little hyperactive and secretive animal: a venomous, egg-laying mammal, with a bill like a duck, feet like an otter, and a tail like a beaver. At times, he would find himself thinking--a mammal that could still lay eggs—how brilliant! What a few Hollywood actresses, or busy professional women would not give to be able to do that trick? Imagine having all your babies at the same time; then instead of   carrying them around in a womb, the eggs could stay in an incubator until they hatch joining the world. Bonding with a fetus over nine months is very much overrated. During the most inconvenient of moments, it kicks and punches an undersized bladder like a punching bag. Then when ready, it pries the cervix and hips unmercifully apart, while pushing its seven and a half pounds of mass through an otherwise perfectly formed vagina. Mothers that say they enjoyed the entire experience are lying: or, have very bad short-term memory. The egg laying strategy of the platypus is much better. The bonding can take place, just as well, as the young begins to suckle a tit. On the funnier side, Stone was convinced the platypus was a creature designed by distant ancestors who were smoking pot while debating and making up the rules of evolution that would ultimately control the beginnings of this universe. Alternatively, he was sure aliens, visiting from a parallel universe, had dropped this animal on the Earth, as a joke, just to screw with the heads of scientists here, who already knew everything there was to know. A breather, or in other words, a vacation to Stone was when there was time for him to learn and get closer to the nature he enjoyed: that was how he played. That was the cause behind his status as a cast-a-way. He wanted to play. The Universe had other plans.

It was September when he, Janet, and *Spiritus* set sail south out of the Niger Delta, headed for Patagonia's and Chile's December summer. They would round Cape Horn so Stone could earn his sailor's badge, a golden earring shaped like a sword in the left ear. Afterward, they visited the Galapagos Islands where Janet had to leave unexpectedly.

Stone and *Spiritus* continued on, sailing down to Easter Island, afterward crossing over to Pitcairn Island, where the mutineers of the HMAV Bounty landed. They set sail towards   Tahiti when an off-season storm caught them in its grips, blowing them far off their intended course.

Both apparently had survived the storm. It was a new day. Their adventure had not ended: it was merely detoured for the moment. There was still a lifetime of opportunities remaining and a lifetime of days and nights one should not waste a minute of on mediocrity. Thus far, there was no harm done.

Nevertheless, for now, on this sun parched pebble filled beach, Stone had a raging thirst. It was apparent to him that his energy was not sufficient to swim towards the *Spiritus,* where freshwater, probably, still remained in storage tanks. Instead, he started to walk barefooted towards the forested side of the mountain. Clouds at the top indicated to Stone that there was an abundance of moisture and indeed gravity insured that it would flow down to the mountains base at some point. At one time in his career, he charged people for that kind of information.

Even though there was no indication of recent volcanic activity on this side of the island, there were no less than three small vents he could see spewing either steam or other gases into the surrounding atmosphere. The vents were at least halfway up the mountain's side.

Stone, a geologist with additional degrees in biology, recently turned his interests towards studying cosmology and the origins of the universe. He concentrated on the mechanisms of evolution. He is an oceanographer with a robust understanding of land-based hydrologic cycles; that is, he knows a few things about how water flows. The side of the mountain in front of him, overgrown with gigantic trees and succulent plants, requires vast amounts of fresh water in order to thrive. All he had to do was follow the path of those trees down to the mountains base and there should be a supply of fresh water. He remembered a question one of his professors put on a test. It took him four years of undergraduate study, and three years of graduate research, to receive his qualifications and professional license that allowed him to charge others for answering the question: "What direction does water flow?" The obvious answer, of course, is always downhill.

Then sure enough, as Stone walked down the beach towards the terminal point of the vegetation, he observed that the beach in front of him recently eroded away by an overflowing stream. He could tell the cut was fresh; the edges in the sand were still sharp and well defined. Wind and rain had not yet rounded off the edges. More than likely, the same storm that caused him to shipwreck caused the ephemeral stream to flow. Stone turned to walk up towards the mountain along the now dry steam bed.

After walking about three hundred meters into the forests interior, Stone happened upon a crystal-clear pool fed by waterfalls. The water was not overflowing into the ocean via the riverbed he had just walked over. Instead, the water was seeping into the substrates surrounding the pond. Those substrates were similar, but smaller than those round pebbles found on the beach: these, blown here from the beach, by stormy winds. They were similar to the Oolitic sands found on the shorelines of Key Biscayne, the Bahamas Islands, or the Great Salt Lake of Utah. Instead of the water flowing over the surface to the ocean, it was seeping into and recharging the surface groundwater before it ultimately reached the shoreline and mixed with the ocean's water.

No matter the sands consistency, for now the curiosity had to be put on hold; Stone was dying of thirst and needed water. His training got him this far, now his lust for water took over. He plunged head first into the cool refreshing water and swallowed his fill before floating back to the surface. This clear fresh water replenished continuously. Harmful amebas that could kill humans, does not lurk in waters such as these. He did not care about any of the little critters that he might have swallowed; stomach acids would kill them. It was amebas crawling up a nose, infesting the brain, which gave him pause. Those, however, at least the ones he was familiar with, lived in hot stagnate waters found in isolated lakes and ponds. Those were not here.

Another test passed. His thirst quenched for the moment. Nonetheless, it would still be hours or days before he was truly up to par. This fresh pool of water offered the gift of rebirth and yet another opportunity for Stone to fulfill his purpose.

Eventually he pulled himself out of the pool and walked to a coconut tree. Perhaps if a coconut crab was opening a nut he could take it: he had no such luck. Instead, he gathered a few freshly fallen coconuts.

Stone began to ponder, slightly disgusted; contemplating what he was willing to do. The thought caused him to pause. At times, he envied those who thought in black and white. They never questioned their actions. They were always right, because their decisions always centered on their own needs. They could easily take the coconut away from the hard working crab, without regard for its well-being. Not Stone, he had to question and measure every decision. Life is about respecting the journey of all sentient beings. When a person holds the heart of a dying friend in their hands, or even that of a stranger, a person learns the hard way, life is not about them; life is about service to others. That is the immutable secret of happiness. These are lessons one learns on the battlefield where decisions are never about self, they are about the team and the team's goal. Stone's immediate dilemma on the island was he, a stronger bigger animal, was willing to steal from a weaker one, solely for the purpose of survival. He was being lazy. There were other more sustainable choices. If he were to steal food from the crabs, they would eventually starve and die. They could all die, and he left without a valuable source of protein. There had to be a better way. Nevertheless, why was this predicament, any different from the armed African rebels, the psychopathic mafia gangsters, or the corrupt government officials stealing from those less aggressive: those that simply choose to live a more social lifestyle within a community? The only difference being, he justified to himself, was that he stood poised on the edge of death: gathering food that used the least amount of his remaining energy was paramount to his survival. Yes, he may soon eat the little monsters for his own benefit, anyway; but at least he remained mindful of what he was doing, and from his species point of view, it was necessary. All decisions had to consider future consequences. From the crabs point of view it simply sucked, but that is nature. Perhaps that is how rebels, corrupt officials, and gangsters justified their deeds—that is nature: big fish eating littler fish. Understanding the balance and where we all fit in as a species, is important to every person's and every thing's survival. Working out equitable solutions and working towards a common purpose, that is what separates gangsters and other lower life parasites, from human beings.

At this very moment, Stone just needed protein, minerals, and carbohydrates to replenish the fats and energy he lost over the last few days at sea. His instincts were taking over and driving him to do what he must to stay alive. At this moment, it was the survival of the fittest: decisions like these drive evolution. Peeling open coconuts by one's self may not be the most efficient decision, but it is the easiest solution for now.

Stone found some volcanic rocks. They were obsidian. Obsidian forms when molten lava flies into the air during volcanic eruptions and cools almost instantly before it hits the ground. It looks like black shinny glass when broken apart. Primitive man had been using obsidian for thousands of years to form tools that made survival easier. He started chipping the igneous rocks to form a hand axe: A skill he learned while on an archeological dig in Portales, New Mexico mucking around on the famous Clovis Point site.

The newly formed stone axe easily cut away the tough and stringy coconut husk. With the nut exposed, he gave a final blow to its center and milk began to spill out over his hand. Stone drank what remained and then cut into the nut to eat the meat. He was not full, but after a few more coconuts, he began to feel a little better. He would need lots of protein soon to help overcome the effects of heat and the stress.

Two more coconuts were split open. Stone left those on the grown for the little monsters that he knew were in the trees and under the dense scrubs, waiting for him to stop moving about. If given a chance, he knew they would clip off a hunk of his hide with their powerful oversized front claws. What he did may have seemed like an act of kindness, but indeed, it was a survival strategy. He wanted the little monsters fat and relaxed in case he could not find other sources of food. It was likely that one would be eating the other very soon. Perhaps, he just remembered, as he does with Stone Crabs, only the claws need to be taken. Afterwards he could leave the crabs opened coconuts to eat, and soon after next shedding their exoskeletons, the claws would grow back. That seemed like a good sustainable trade; at least for him. Other than the fact that the crabs would be alive to live another day, it would still suck for the crabs: still, it would be better than the alternative. Stone would become "King Leopold II, the thief of renewable claws," instead of human hands.

He spotted geckos scampering under the fallen coconut fronds. These animals repopulated rapidly, and quickly adapted to environmental changes. Some species are parthenogenic, which means the female is capable of reproducing without copulating with a male. A handy tool when you want to build a family on an isolated Pacific island. Using both hands Stone captured a few. After ripping their heads off, he ate their bodies--entrails and all. He needed the protein so he could quickly rebuild his energy. The geckos were not happy about this at all. Nevertheless, strategies for leaving this island paradise required a rested body and an alert mind: protein was required.

Later, after a good rest and more water, he would begin to explore the surrounding area and start to look for fruits, nuts, and animal life that would supplement his diet. Yes, the less then ingenious coconut crabs would be top on the menu and soon. Six to seven pounds of sweet crabmeat cooked with bananas can go a long way towards healing a human body. Now, however, he needed sleep.

Stone rested on top of the white little pebbles that lined the shore of the cool clear pond and began to drift off: for the moment, he was safe from storms and angry rich guys who wanted him dead. The threat of the little monsters did not bother him; the first one to pinch him would be rewarded with a bath in hot boiling water-- without feelings of guilt.

Before falling off into a deep blissful sleep, tapes kept repeating in his head, over and over again they kept showing the GIECO gecko holding a gun pointed towards Stone, demanding that he keep his hands in the air and don't dare move. Stone laughed aloud before passing out; another potential partner for the 9 Tomatoes a Day purpose based marketing programs.

If humanity were simply animals, it would be nothing out of the ordinary to steal from others, to make them work as slaves, or to needlessly murder people, as a means of taking their land and property. Humans, however, have the gift of larger brains with the ability to reason and work towards a common purpose. It is time they begin to use that gift. It is time for humanity to exit the sandbox and reach for the stars, in search of their highest potential.

3

THE SURVEY

When Stone finally woke up, there was still a few hours of sunlight remaining. He started to walk along the base of the mountain and found a path that leads to a rock outcrop poised high above the forest canopy: perched from up there, he might be able to see the size of this pacific rock in the middle of nowhere.

It was hot, he was still weak, but he continued forward tenaciously, up a path obviously made by some animal. After slipping a few times, and grabbing onto an unfriendly thorny branch to steady his balance, he made it up to the cliff's ledge. The efforts reward was amazing: in front of him laid a forest canopy of dense tall trees surrounded by a vast blue ocean. He saw, mixed within the trees, tall cacao trees used to make chocolate; he saw bananas, plantains, dates, and even more coconuts. There were fruit trees he had never seen before: there would be plenty of time to experiment with them. A wide coral reef, with smaller islands intermixed, rimmed the entire main island.

A tall mountain was behind him; a billowy mist of clouds rolled around by a gentle pacific breeze crowned its peak. One day soon, he would climb above the clouds to see what was there, but not today. It was nearing dark and he needed to make camp. Tomorrow he would wake and explore the island's far side.

As he headed back, a feral pig ran by. The sow had eight little piglets tagging behind. Now he knew sailors had visited this island before. In the days of great sailing ships, it was normal for the captains to leave animals behind on small islands: that way, if a crew ran out of food, or were ship wrecked, there would be fresh meat available. He also saw signs of large tortoise. There would be no shortage of protein and carbohydrates on this island. At least he would eat well.

The mystery, however, remained. Why the island did not show up on the charts? Perhaps, it had. Perhaps, he simply lost his position on the charts. The storm was fierce and violent, making it impossible for him to check the global positioning equipment. Eventually seawater damaged the equipment beyond repair. The presence of the pigs may mean the island is closer to a shipping lane than once thought.

Walking a little deeper into the forest, Stone found bananas, ripe and ready to eat. Using his stone axe he struck the tree's trunk multiple times, causing it to fall down. He pulled one banana off the bunch and peeled back the bright yellow skin. When he tasted it, the meat was sweet and firm. He needed the carbohydrates and potassium to increase his energy level. He threw the rest of the bunch on his shoulders, then began making his way back to the pond.

When Stone returned to his base, he pulled apart palm fronds weaving them into rope, for hanging the bananas from a tree branch. Otherwise, the little monsters would have them eaten by morning.

With the camp organized, also knowing where he would sleep, he stripped down and jumped into the clear waters of the pond. He swam to the waterfall and sat under it; cooling off and rehydrating, while contemplating his predicament. It was not awful, but over time, it could be lonely. He would have to busy himself everyday in order to keep his mind off that fact. He began by thinking about tomorrow's chores.

First thing in the morning, before he walked to the other side, he would collect wood and pile it up, to build a signal fire. It would alert a passing plane, or a ship, to his presence when lit. A week, or more, will pass before someone reports his failure to dock in Tahiti. It could be a month before anyone even decides to mount a search party. A plane could spot the *Spiritus* on the rocks. That would give them cause to search this is-land. Then again, how far off the shipping channels is this island? Stone had no idea. The presence of the cacao trees told him he was well within 20 degrees south of the equator. Those trees do not grow outside of that range north or south of the equator. He already confirmed from the constellations he was still in the southern hemisphere.

Stone pulled himself from the pool and began to use his axe to cut down fresh palm fronds. He laid them over the pebbles for bedding. Tonight he would sleep well. It was the first time in days, he had chosen to sleep; instead of being forced to pass out from exhaustion.

After the moon raced across the night sky, it was now early morning with the first rays of morning sunlight creeping into the base camp.

"Ouch! Damn-it that hurt," Stone screamed, torn from a deep sleep. As the sun began to rise, one daring little monster thought it would take one of Stone's little toes for breakfast. After

Stone screamed, the crab just stood there with its claws extended upwards, exactly like a cowboy holding pistols.

Stone admired bravery, and instead of killing the little shit, he would eat it, a little at a time. Stone grabbed both of its front claws holding them steady until the crab finally gave them up, just as they would do for any other predator: it is their survival mechanism. This was how Stone would begin his second day on the island: Fresh crabmeat, bananas, and coconut meat. Tomorrow morning he would have the ancient Inca drink 'chocolat' made from the cacao (coco) tree. It was as close to coffee as he was going to get for a long time.

Stone limped around, trying to keep his toe out of the pebbles, while gathering some twigs, moss, and other types of kindling. Once, he was the best fire maker in his old Baptist church youth group, the Royal Ambassadors. He prided himself on never having to use a match to start the campfires. He hated going to church, or to Sunday school, where they relentlessly tried to indoctrinate him with their religious dogma, but he always looked forward to the RA group where instructors taught practical survival skills like a Boy Scout would learn.

It was not long before a small fire ignited, and the bananas, the coconut, and the crabmeat, wrapped in banana leaves, began steaming in the left over coconut juice: Stone's first cooked meal in a week.

The geckos looked a little less stressed knowing this giant had turned his appetite toward other foods. Once again, Stone could hear their chirps, perhaps crying out to the others the all clear signal.

After his battle with Stone, the little clawless monster had climbed a tree and was most certainly broadcasting abuses that only the other crabs could understand: perhaps the little clicks and squeaks were warnings to leave that giant's toes alone, if they knew what was good for them.

After breakfast, Stone walked along the beach and piled up bits and pieces of driftwood, and gathered old dried palm trunks to make a signal fire. Later he would build a small fire next to the big pile and keep it burning. If he needed to light the big pile, as a ship or plane passed by, the hot smaller fire would be there, at the ready.

After gathering all the dry-wood he could find for the signal fire, Stone stripped down and swam out to the *Spiritus* to survey the damage. When he got there, it was like visiting a sick relative in the hospital. All anyone can do is try to comfort the infirmed. Other forces have control of their destiny. There was a gaping hole on the side of the boat; fortunately, it was well above the water line. It would be possible to refloat the *Spiritus* and then perhaps make repairs. Again, that project is for another day, far into the future, when Stone's strength and endurance returns. Nevertheless, it was a relief to know it was possible.

He began to round up supplies to make his life comfortable on land. He looked around for the EPIRP, but could not locate it. Then he remembered a wave took it away during the first night of the storm. It is probably still out there floating, leading boats, and aircraft in an entirely different direction, away from his pending rescue. Stone entered the cabin. It was disorienting at first. The boat was on its side; he had to walk on the lockers and cabinets as he moved about. Everything was scattered. He went to the galley and collected whatever cooking pots and pans he could find, and put spices and dry goods in a cooler. For entertainment, while sitting near fires at night, he collected a few cases of undamaged red wine that would help him pass time, as he continued to contemplate his predicament. He found his Leatherman; a devise any good sailor should never be without—it also had an all important corkscrew, and beer opener.

Stone carried all the collected items outside. He went to the front deck and unlatched the life raft; then before inflating it, tossed the raft into the water. After fastening the raft to the side of the boat, the food and cookery were loaded. He made another trip to the inside in search for more treasures.

He rounded up a hammock, some more clothing and found hiking boots. He recovered his 45 Colt automatic in a waterproof case. He had been carrying that gun with him since his military technical school. It has seen all the horrors he had seen, and is partly responsible for his continued existence. There may not be any pirates on the island, but the gun will save a lot of energy the next time one of the monsters attempts to eat his toes. A water proof, hand held VHF was found with a line of sight, transmission and reception range, of six to twelve miles, just in case a ship or plane were passing by. The other electronics were fried. The chart plotter containing all the navigational data was lost. The saltwater had long ago seeped into the covers, corroding the circuit boards beyond repair.

The ship's batteries had busted out of their lockers, draining acid everywhere. They would not be of any use.

Oddly enough, the diesel fuel had stayed in the tanks; the diesel could power the generator. Stone needed a method to float the power station to shore. That would come later. Right now, he collected a few gallons of fuel into jugs for the signal fire. He gathered up a steel hand axe that would replace is handmade tool, found a hunting knife, and a waterproof flash light that required no batteries.

Stone found his spear gun; it had seen many oceans over the years. In his early military days on the island of Crete, Stone and his friend Stephanos would dive in the Aegean Sea that fronted their homes in Chersonasu. They would shoot chubby grouper, catch crafty octopus, and hand grab stealthy flipper tailed lobsters. It was there Stone learned to survive on the sea. It was also how Stephanos lived like a king in a small village that was otherwise very poor: it was how Stone, who made $5000 a year in the military, could afford to live off base; that is before his Base Commander and the Air Force made it a little bit more affordable--and profitable. All he had to do in return for the improved lifestyle was to expose an enterprise trading drugs for guns, and avoid a bullet in the brain during the process. Stone survived, but many did not. Moreover, those that died, did not die for a cause, they died because of greed and corruption. It was on Crete that Stone learned, a bonfire on the beach, with a pot full of fresh steamed seafood, a bottle of home-made wine, and a loaf of hot fresh bread, shared with good friends, was more valuable than all the gold a bank could hold.

With everything loaded in the raft, Stone finally collected a few sails and enough rope to hang canopies over the camp that would provide cover from the afternoon rains. He was ready to float the first load to the shore.

Stone untied the raft. Afterward, he tied the tether around his waist. With his treasures in tow, he started to swim back to the shore. Prior to diving in the water, he had put on flippers, a diving mask, and a snorkel. As he made his way through the clear sea-water, he watched out for any signs of edible sea life that lived in and around the rocks. It was plentiful. Gorgonians (Sea Fans) and large sponges were everywhere. Anywhere there was a spot to at-tach, there were large sea anemone dangling from rocks, with clown fish darting in and out of the anemone's poisonous tentacles. The antennae of spiny lobster were protruding out of every crack and crevice. As Stone dived underwater to look into rock crevasses, he found shovel nosed lobster clinging to the tops. Red fish and grouper were bountiful. The telltale signs pointing toward dens of large shy octopus were prevalent. Most of the octopuses in these waters are strange and sometimes venomous. Nonetheless, there may be one edible species. Scallops attached to rocks were every-where. Sea Urchins were plentiful. Urchins were not his favorite food, but they certainly outdo headless gecko. Stone would not be going hungry for many years to come. All he would have to do is share the bounty in this lagoon, with the large sharks that have been eyeing him since he first swam to the *Spiritus*.

When he got to shore, Stone unloaded the raft and carried his goodies to the oasis next to the pond. Tonight there would be a modernized home: a hammock hung high above the reach of the toe eating monsters, a canvas stretched out overhead to keep the rain off, a fire to cook a hot tropical meal, and a waterfall to create a soothing background noise from which one could easily fall asleep.

After dragging the now empty raft to the dune line and tying it to a palm, in case the wind picks up, or a storm blows by, it was still early morning according to the sun; noon was still a few hours away.

Stone went back to the camp and put on khaki pants and a pair of hiking boots; and then he filled a water pouch also collected from the boat. With water, a few bananas, and some power bars, he managed to salvage, Stone began the expedition towards the other side of the island.

During his walk, he collected ripe nuts from the cacao trees and cut them open to retrieve the rich cacao seeds. While doing so, he also thought to himself that the wine would not last forever. He would soon have to start fermenting the coconuts and bananas into only god knows what, as long as it helps to dull the long lonely nights on top of a rock in the middle of the ocean. He had a thirty-gallon water pouch salvaged from the boat specifically for that purpose.

Altogether, it took two long hot hours to reach the other side of the island. When he arrived, it was worth every step taken in the hot sticky forest. In front of him was a vast open cove camouflaged with an assortment of exotic fruit and nut bearing trees. It was as if someone had deliberately planted them into a grove. There was a plentiful amount of mature bamboo with shoots as thick as his legs. It was a beautiful oasis. A deep winding canal connected the ocean inlet to an open, calm, and deep interior bay. The clear green water was full of corals and fish. Next to the bay was a large opening leading to a cave at the base of the volcano. It was over 30 meters (ninety feet) high and that wide again.

Stone walked inside. The interior cavern was immense. Portions of the ceiling had fallen in and served as skylights providing enough illumination to see every detail the cave had to offer. There were three waterfalls starting at the caverns ceiling, which fell into huge catch basins formed in the rocks, after years of erosion. The light from above, shined down through the water making it seem as though there were underwater lights. The water appeared hazy, due to the mixing of salinities, as the fresh water mixed with the incoming seawater. Within those mixing zones, nothing was in focus, but Stone could just barely make out images made by numerous schools of fish. Within this massive cave were smaller caves that lined the back walls and looked like they once could have served as individual homes. Upon further inspection, one cave contained a skeleton of human remains partially covered by dirt that must have fallen from the cave walls over the years. From the etchings on the wall, it appeared this cast-a-way lived there for a long time. Words carved into the cave wall just above the skull read:

Such happiness one finds in the quietness proffered by nature's bosom; such profound sadness one endures, with no one to share it.

Abraham Evens, Bosun's Mate, HMS Delfe, 1669

Stone was considering if he was looking at his destiny. What was Mr. Evens' story? There are no records of British ships in this area during the sixteen hundreds. In fact, Charles II had only restored the monarchy in 1660, at which time he also rebuilt the Royal Navy. What would history be like if Evens would have returned to Britain; whose thunder would have been taken? Dead men, unknown and cast-a-away, make no history. Stone nodded a few times, empathizing with Evens' words, and then he went back to work.

Looking at the bay inside the larger cavern, Stone thought to himself, if he could just refloat the *Spiritus,* this could be the perfect place to bring it and attempt repairs. Mr. Evens might enjoy the company, and seeing what a modern boat looks like after 342 years of progress. Things were looking up. Stone had just found a cheap waterfront condominium in the middle of the Pacific Ocean on a desolate island. He could not have been happier. Over the next few weeks, he would move his base camp to this area. He could use Evens' company. Somehow, he would figure out how to refloat the *Spiritus*: getting her to this cave, and starting the work was now a priority.

During his two-hour hike, back to base camp, Stone began to see this desolate island for something more than a dry platform in the middle of the ocean. It truly was a paradise. It had virtually any-thing someone could ask for except companionship: there was Evens, but he would prove too quiet: there were the toe stealing monsters, but Stone was thinking more about the human kind, like Janet for instance. She had gotten ill when they reached the Gala-pagos and had to return to the States for medical treatment. After-ward, she was going to meet him in Sydney, Australia. But what now?

Janet was his interpreter in Haiti. She became an important part of a global team that showed the world it was possible to build farm cooperatives that would end poverty for millions of people. She later boarded the *Spiritus* with Stone and sailed away without any consideration or care about their next destination. They were just enjoying the moment and the anticipation of where the sum-mer breeze might take them next. Their trip ended in the Niger Del-ta but Stone asked that she return to the states until he got a better handle on the problems they found there. The Delta was a danger-ous lawless place to live. Even the Nigerian army never entered this area, unless they were in mass and well armed.

With the job completed, Janet returned and they both once again took sail: this time simply for the pleasure. They would travel to Australia together via Cape Horn. Janet would like this island. It offered much. Maybe one day, she would see it with him.

Stone got to the base camp and immediately started a fire. He was beginning to shake from hunger. There was a little light left over so he grabbed his mask, fins, and snorkel, and then snatched-up his spear gun as he walked to the oceans shore. He waded in and immediately swam over to the rocks where he last saw the lobsters hiding earlier in the morning. He caught three large ones with his bare hands and speared a large grouper. While there, he also pried a dozen scallops off the rocks. It was all he could carry. It was simply all he could eat.

He brought his bounty back to the camp, where he then cut down a few fresh banana leaves. He wrapped the seafood in the leaves with some coconut meat, dates, bananas, and some coconut juice. Although this combination tasted wonderful, he was thinking some native herbs would help to break up the monotony. For the moment, however, this was perfect.

More banana leaves covered the fire, and then the package of seafood with more leaves topped that. It was smoky, but it smelt good. It would not take long; the meat inside needed to steam only minutes before it would be dinnertime.

Stone used the few minutes to clean up. He stripped down, jumped into the pool, and swam a few laps. When he got out, it was time to eat. He cleared the fire of the banana leaves and added some more wood. He opened a bottle of wine and began his feast. Above him watching from a safe distant was a pissed off clawless monster clinging to a palm tree. Stone looked up and said, "Stop fussing; if you think about it, it could have been a lot worse for you."

He was again sated, as well as tired. He was starting to feel more energetic. He was going to sleep now because he had worked hard, not because of stress. He crawled into his hammock and began to stare at the stars pondering their eternal history; those were his last thoughts before falling asleep.

As part of the initiation rituals into the Cosa Nostra, a perspective member holds a piece of paper stained with the person's blood; written on it is an oath of loyalty. It is then set on fire. The holder may not drop the paper; he must hold it until it completely burns. Sometimes the Universe does something like that to initiate a person into a small club, whose intent is to drive purpose.

4

GALACTIC NIGHTMARE

When Stone awoke hours later, it was still dark. He continued to lie in the hammock watching the clear night sky; bright glittering specks littered the view. There were more stars than he had ever seen before. There was a rare type of activity and excitement in this sky. Everything in space seemed to have movement beyond the normal. The Milky Way was amazing to behold, the Southern Cross was clearly visible above the horizon. How small and insignificant Stone felt in the mist of these wandering giants within the vastness of space. How ashamed he sometimes felt on behalf of his arrogant brothers and sisters, who do not stop to consider their place in the universe; otherwise, too consumed with the collection of worthless trinkets and knick-knacks. To wake up under the vastness of the universe was good for any human's ego. It reminds them to be careful; that no matter how powerful they may appear here on earth, the heavens can always crash down on them from the top, while microscopic bacteria and virus can destroy them from the bottom.

This night was extraordinary; Stone had awakened to the most active meteor shower he had ever seen. Every few seconds a dozen or so meteors would scream across the night sky, like bats with their tails on fire.

He was searching to find constellations that would give him a clue where we was after three full days and nights of fighting a storm that left him completely disoriented. Fortunately, even without his electronics, Stone still had a sexton that would put him as close to his current position as any advanced technology. He had found a few paper charts that might help him. With that information, he could plot a course. If he was unable to re-float and re-pair the *Spiritus*, he could build a sailing raft from bamboo, and then sail it to the nearest civilization. From there he could find a way to get the *Spiritus* back into the water and doing what she does best with her captain.

In the night sky, there was one star much brighter than the others were. It was simply too bright and growing in size too fast to be something ordinary. Something about the star made Stone feel uneasy. It seemed to get bigger and bigger. He stood up from his hammock. Stone rubbed his eyes thinking it was just age or stress, and perhaps they were simply out of focus due to the recent day's events. Soon he could not even look at it for its brightness. It was then a feeling of impending doom swam over him. Out of all the places on the Earth; why this little island where he was forced to take refuse?

Stone determined it had to be a meteor and in seconds, it would be landing somewhere very close. There was no other explanation. Seeing all the other meteors crashing to earth confirmed his theory. It was going to land close by; otherwise, he would have been able to see its trail as it burned-up entering the atmosphere.

When Stone could finally see the meteor's tail, it was too late. Just a few milliseconds later, the meteor crashed into the side of the mountain followed by large boom. What followed would change his life forever.

A violent explosion ejecting rock, gas, and fire tore-out from the side of the mountain. When Stone finally opened his eyes the entire area around the impact zone was on fire, and everything was a-glow with a blue-green luminescence containing a yellowish-white glitter that reminded him of St. Elmo's fire. The glitter sprang from the edges of everything Stone surveyed. It was as though little strings of Christmas lights created an outline of every tree, stick, rock, or crab. Even Stone looked as though he was standing under an ultraviolet light: his frame, even his hands, appeared to glowing with the little specks of light. The sea was on fire with sparkling glitter. The outline of *Spiritus'* rigging could be seen from shore.

There was no doubt that Stone was standing in the middle of an electromagnetic event, but what did that mean? He knew from the rocks that the island was volcanic in its origins. He had discovered numerous small deposits of pitchblende in the cracks of rocks. Earlier he discovered a boulder of pitchblende, two feet in diameter. Uraninite, or pitchblende, is a major source of uranium that he had seen once before in the Oklo mines of Gabon, West Africa. That was the only place in the world where there use to be a natural nuclear fission reactor operating just below the Earth's surface: a reaction only nature was involved in, not man.

Uranium can only be formed naturally in the high temperatures found in time frames just before supernovae explode apart: a place where there are immeasurable pressures caused by gravitational forces that result in temperatures reaching millions of degrees: this is where all naturally occurring elements with atomic weights higher than iron are formed.

When these higher atomic weight, and sometimes radioactive, elements disperse into space after the supernova explodes, they mix with other gigantic dust clouds similar to the Eagle or Orion nebulas that span many light years across: one light year is 10 Trillion Kilometers or the distance light travels over a span of a year at 300,000 kilometers per second.

When the resulting dust particles begin to accrete, they first form new stars that have 'dust disks' surrounding them. It is from those dust disks that planets begin to form. That is why all the soil on Earth contains uranium with concentrations between 0.7 to 11 parts per million. The seawater contains on average 3 parts per billion of uranium.

Many scientists theorize that the heat from the radioactive decay of uranium, thorium, and potassium-40 in the Earth's inner-core is one of the multiple reasons why the outer-core is liquid. The outer-core drives the convection currents in the mantle: and those convention currents cause the continental and oceanic plates to grow, subside, and collide into one another. That is why this island, like the Hawaiian and Ascension Islands, exists in the middle of the Pacific or Atlantic Oceans with nothing else around them. They grow from hot spots in the ocean's crust or near spreading zones where volcanoes rise above the sea surface to begin building new land. From Stone's point of view, there had to be a higher than normal concentration of uranium in the liquid mantle that formed this island. That was the only source from which Pitchblende could form.

Somehow in the mix of events, the protons from the meteor collided with the Uraninite at super-sonic speeds. When the atoms reached a critical mass, it resulted in some type of explosion forming a type of electromagnetic storm, instead of a nuclear explosion. It was a mystery. Why there was not sufficient heat from the explosion to vaporize the entire island is anyone's guess. Apparently, the meteor and the plasma surrounded it were not traveling fast enough to reach the required energy to initiate nuclear fission. Perhaps, fortunately, there simply was not the right mix of elements for a nuclear event.

Nonetheless, there were also multiple strata of rock on the island comprised of relic coral reefs apparently lifted out of the ocean as the volcanoes broke through the oceans crust. The presence of the corals situated so high above the current shoreline indicated to him that this island did not rise quickly but that it must have taken thousands of years to grow to its current size.

Some reef corals are capable of growing 15 centimeters (6 inches) in a year. Larger corals such as star coral and brain coral grow considerably slower, typically only 1/8 inch to 3/4 inch per year. As old corals die, new ones usually settle and grow over the dead skeletons. Many generations of settlement, competition, growth and death result in structures like the Great Barrier Reef in Australia, which is hundreds of feet thick and millions of years old. If Stone remained stuck on this island for too long, he would soon be figuring out just how long this volcanic island had been blocking the path of sea weary sailors: that is, if he survives whatever just happened.

Over the last few days, Stone noticed steam rising from the forest on the sides of the mountain. It was there he discovered thermal vents. He found a mixture of volcanic rocks rich in uranium, deposits of concentrated Pitchblende, and the thermal vents known to yield other unique metals and mineral compounds, with sulfur and potassium in them. All those combined with the carbon rich biogenic minerals derived from the sea and on land, all mixing with the superheated meteorite of unknown composition, colliding into the mountain at supersonic speeds, created instantaneously unimaginable pressures and even higher temperatures. It would be anyone's guess as to what the chemical compositions of the resulting gases and dust were.

Experience shows, the prior mineralogy of the mountain, as well as the conditions at the time of impact create source areas of radioactive minerals. It happened once before in the Oklo mines of West Africa. If the concentration of uranium were high enough (who knew what the meteorite brought with it) a small peculiar type of nuclear reaction could have just happened. If nothing else, it was certainly natures answer for a dirty bomb. Stone had just stood witness to the entire spectacular event: but he may not live long enough to tell anyone about it. It was like that joke; a preacher shot

18 holes in one, but could not tell anyone about it, because he was suppose to be in church on a Sunday. God toyed and laughed at the delinquent preacher: was God toying and laughing at Stone?

It had now been a few minutes since the event; he began to feel hot and itchy all over. He started to get dizzy and vomited, just before he dropped to his knees and passed out. It was just what he needed after a few days of recuperation from the storm: more stress.

Nothing is known independently, everything exists because of its interactions with the great unity called the cosmos.

5

THE MORNING AFTER

Over 24 hours rolled by since the explosion, and Stone spent all that time passed out on his back. He began to stir and move about. Very slowly, he put his hand to his forehead and turned over so he could get up on his knees. He looked around and saw that most of the vegetation was turning brown or yellow. Everything was dying around him. All the little monsters were dead or hiding in their deep underground burrows, he could not tell. The waterfalls had stopped flowing.

Stone did not dare rise to his feet. He felt sick to his stomach and he became even dizzier with every movement he made. He crawled over to the pond and rolled into the water. It was no longer cool. It was becoming stagnated without the cool refreshing water once supplied by the waterfalls. Still Stone drank what he could. It helped a little. He remained in the water for a little while longer trying to regain his bearings and trying to understand what is happening to him. He feared the worst. He got half way out of the water before passing out again with his head falling on the soft round pebbles.

Every few hours he would wake and try to drink. He forced himself to eat one of the remaining power bars, and a now brown and rotting banana. In the end, however, all he really wanted to do was pass out.

Over two days had passed, during which he had frequent headaches and diarrhea. At first, he thought it was the geckos, he once again began to eat out of convenience; or maybe it was too many coconuts, the rotting bananas, or bad water. He realized his worse fears when his pubic, head, and body hair started to fall out in clumps. It was obvious; he had been exposed to high doses of radiation, perhaps over 8 Gy. It was possible he would soon die a very horrible death, bleeding from the inside out, as his entrails turned to jelly.

His supply of iodine pills washed overboard with the rest of his medical supplies during the storm. Without the iodine, to rid his body of the radiation poisoning, the symptoms would be difficult to counteract. If he had the strength, he could capture and eat whatever shellfish was available. Sea-salt was the only other reliable source of iodine he could imagine on the island. All the alternatives would take too much energy, and he was too weak. Furthermore, with exposures higher than 8 Gy, there was no hope. Stone had received a lethal dose of radiation poisoning. As a result, he could only stand for a few minutes before becoming dizzy and falling down once more. Perhaps he could find a way to spare himself this long tortuous death. He sure did not want to stab himself to death with a spike made from bamboo. He always had his Colt 45 magnum; a single bullet would stop all this misery. Perhaps if he had enough strength he could climb to the mountain top and throw his body down to the ragged rocks below: anything but having to shit himself to death while bleeding into his own guts. He was trying to remember where he put the 45: it would be more fitting to end his own life than let anyone else or anything else, take life from him. He would die just as he lived, on his own terms. He began to hear his grandfather singing to him. His grandfather use to sing his mantra as they both fished away lazy days:

Some times when papa and I,
would fish the days away;
he'd lay back on the ground,
look at the sky and say:
In all the things that matter,
you must heed these words I pray;
Live your life with Purpose:
Die with intent...no other way.

Read each word as though,
a monster lives within.
You must question everything,
ignore who call that sin!
Be involved with all that matters,
and avoid the fringe of foes.
Live your life with purpose:
Die with intent...no other way

Life's too short for simple think;
it took years to compete.
Life's too short for mediocrity,
the sands of time complete.
Keep building up the castles,
leave footprints sure to stick.
Live your life with purpose:
Die with intent...no other way.

There's no gold found in heaven,
no pockets found in hell,
the only riches that we take,
are the deeds we leave behind.
So stop your foolish hording,
and help your friends to live, so
Live your life with purpose;
Die with intent...no other way.

Some days when papa and I,
would fish the days away,
He'd lay back on the ground,
look at the sky then say,
in all the things that matter,
heed these words I pray;
Live your life with Purpose:
Die with intent...no other way.

You must live your life with Purpose:
Die with intent—there is...no other way.

Stone was becoming delirious and disoriented. He tried to eat a coconut but they tasted foul. Nothing seemed to taste right. Everything tasted awful. Then again, he remained very hungry and thirsty. He stumbled out to the ocean; all about him was nothing but dead rotting fish and crabs. Even the seabirds were not eating this free meal.

He fell to his knees in frustration, starting to feel, once again, the agonizing effects of hunger, thirst, excessive heat, and the fatigue that follows. He started to fall asleep on the beach...**but that is when he found himself at Alfredo's restaurant!**

Stone was beginning to understand. All he had to do was envision a place, want to go there, and somehow he would end up in that place. That was too cool: too odd. Things like that only happen to comic book characters, not to men of science. Now he needed time to think and understand what this all meant: for the moment, and for his future. He thought about Alfredo's and again--instantaneously--he was at the bar.

"Sassolino, what you doing there? You scare the crap-pa out of me doing that. Now I have to wash my hands again. My goodness, how you do that? I didn't hear the bell. You wanna eat something?"

"Give me a beer Alfredo, per favore, and an order of chicken picatta."

There he was; it was not a dream. It was, nevertheless, as close to a miracle as he would ever let himself believe: a miracle provided by a freakish natural event—Brilliant! All he apparently had to do was think about some place he wanted to be and he would instantly, in a flash, jump there. How could that happen? It was impossible, but here again, it was happening.

Stone took a sip of the cold Italian beer: Peroni was an acquired taste, one that required you to return repeatedly; or your legs would break. It went well with the chicken picatta with extra lemon, garlic, and capers over fettuccini.

Stone cut into the succulent chicken and put it into his mouth. It was one of those tastes that once you had it, you will never forget: the memorable mixtures of garlic, lemon, capers, and olive oil blended with an obscene amount of real butter to add to the otherwise heart healthy meal.

As he allowed the flavors to blend and absorb into his mouth he watched with concern as Alfredo dropped things and bumped into others. His hands were shaking. Stone had to ask:

"Alfredo, are you ok?"

"Stone, you have been having too many troubles of your own. Thank you."

"No my friend, tell me. What is up?"

"It's-a ok, Sassolino. I have control of it."

"Ok my friend, but you know, anything you need, you know I will be there to help you."

"Sure yes I know this, thank you, you are a good friend, but I have to do this myself."

"Alfredo, I will see you again soon."

After paying this time, Stone walked to the back entrance and opened the door; he jumped back to the island. Now at the island, he walked over to a pile of his things and recovered his old companion, the Colt 45 magnum. He checked it to make sure there were no pebbles inside. The bullets he found loaded were not needed to end his misery after all.

Sometimes, it is best to ride out the pain life dishes out. You never know what the universe has in-store for you and your future: everything a person experiences is a test: how you handle the test frames the meaning for the rest of your life. The wonderful thing about sleep is that every morning, when you recover, it is exactly like being reborn. Every new day is a clean slate. Everything that happened yesterday is gone. You can become anyone or anything new that you desire. You simply have to want it and commit to the goal.

Stone saw 'old no claws' hanging onto a palm a few yards away. Stone shot apart four coconuts that were lying on the ground; blowing them into fragments so there would be easy food for the lucky little monster. To avoid fighting other crabs off, hopefully, the monster would take the pieces into his burrow. Stone also cut the string and let the rotting bunch of bananas fall to the ground. He looked up at the monster and said, "Thanks for the helping hands."

He then thought about his bedroom and jumped back to his home. There he got some cash he kept in a safe, and his spare debit card. He then jumped to the Merritt Square Mall and purchased a cell phone. Stone always paid more for the phones so he was never under a cell company's thumb. If their management continued to screw up and ignored customer service, he simply would change companies. Stone always voted with his wallet. For instance he always choose phones by the way companies handled their conflict mineral policies, divulging to the public their supply chain, and certified that they used only conflict free minerals.

After buying the cell phone, he then jumped to a specialty store and purchased a satellite phone and global internet service for his laptop.

With his new phone, he first called Alfredo to give him the new numbers, just in case he decided to talk; next he called an old reliable friend—Buck. Buck had been with Stone during military missions considered off the books. Without asking a question, Buck dropped everything to help Stone build farms cooperatives in Haiti. In the Niger Delta, Buck took a bullet when both of them tore a terrorist network wide open. Buck had always been dependable, a rare find in a friend. Then Buck was always a danger addict and for some reason, Stone always found himself in the middle of it.

"Stone, where have you been? I had dinner with Janet last night; she said all contact was lost with you and the *Spiritus*. Your EPIRP surfaced days ago but you were nowhere to be found. She is worried to death about you."

"Thanks for reminding me. I have been out of it for a while. Buck I need you to be calm for me over the next few hours. I have a few extraordinary things to tell and show you that may otherwise freak you out. I need you to keep an open mind and just go along with it until you find your balance. I cannot fully explain what if happening to me yet, but I have a few ideas. I need help to find some researchers that can help explain what is going on."

"You know me Stone, point and I jump."

"You have never experienced something like this before Buck. Where are you standing right now?"

"I am in my living room, drinking a beer on the couch."

"Do you have enough beer?"

"Not really, one can never have enough beer, can they?"

"Fine, I will see you in a few seconds."

With that, Stone hung up and jumped to the convenience store that was next door to his house. He walked inside and put $15 on the counter, grabbed the cheapest beer that Buck liked and walked out. Next, when he jumped, Stone was sitting on the couch, right next to Buck.

Buck was looking straight into Stone's eyes. One second Buck was looking at a picture on the distant wall, the next second

Stone's face was right in front of him. Buck jumped sideways as though a jealous husband just entered the room; the opened beer he was holding went flying into the air then crashed onto the wooden floor.

"What the... in Lucifer's name, are you doing? I nearly crapped my pants! Where did you come from! My heart! I have not been that scared since some dink held a loaded gun to my nuts. What the crap?"

"I told you this would be extraordinary. You need to calm down now. Have a cold beer. OK?"

Stone opened a cold Miller in a bottle and handed it to Buck. Buck took a big swallow.

"Yea, yea fine. I will be ok. Give me a second. Shit, what's this about?"

"It's a longer story than we have time for Buck, but the short version is that I was in a bad storm. Later, I shipped wrecked on a deserted island. I was getting along fine: making my way; I even made a few friends; that is, until a meteor hit the side of a volcanic mountain and showered this radioactive stuff all over me. I had some reaction to the radioactivity. I lost my hair, but gained an ability to jump in milliseconds, to anywhere I can think of."

"You're kidding me right?"

Stone reached over, crabbed Bucks arm, and thought about the island beach in front of the *Spiritus*. The next second they both were on the beach.

"Damn it Stone!"

Buck, still in a sitting position, fell backwards onto the pebbles, losing another beer.

"Buck, if you keep doing that, it is going to get expensive: maybe you should put the beer in a container with a lid."

"Then, dang-it, tell me before you go zapping my frigging atoms all over God's creation."

"You want another beer?"

"No...I think I need to sober up a bit for this."

"That's how it works, that is all I know."

"But how: Why?

"Like I said Buck, I have no idea yet. Hold on I want to show you something else."

With that said, Stone reached over for Buck's arm.

"Woe, woe hold on their Flash Gordon, we gonna be flying around again?"

"Yes, we are."

"Just want to prepare myself. Go!"

Both of them jumped to the inside of the cave, located on the other side of the mountain.

"Stone this is amazing, oh my."

"Yea, I am going to try something else. Stay away from this area Buck, it could be dangerous."

Stone then jumped to the *Spiritus*. It was lying at such an angle that if he was careful, he might be able to refloat it without doing further damage.

He positioned himself in the cockpit behind the helm; as he held onto his boat, he thought of the wide-open calm spaces inside the cave. The next second, the *Spiritus* and Stone were in the cave, floating in the water. The *Spiritus* was struggling to right itself before any more water entered the cabin from the hole above the water line.

"Now that's what I am talking about!" yelled Buck. "By any chance did that hurt your back?"

"I didn't know if that was going to work or not. I am learning with each new hour what I can do. Help me tie it up and let's see what we need to get her back in shape."

Stone moved to the foredeck and tossed Buck some lines. Buck pulled the boat closer to the rock ledge where they could install a gantry for loading and unloading the boat. Then Stone walked to the stern and tossed Buck another line.

With the boat secured, Stone tossed another rope to Buck, who pulled the gantry to the shore and secured it. Stone secured the other end of the gantry to the *Spiritus*. Buck walked on the boat for the first time in months.

"You're going to try and fix her in here?"

"Not yet Buck, but can you think of a better place? We are over a thousand miles from the nearest civilization, with a hole in the side large enough to walk through. We have to get some supplies here, and some workers that can help. She does not have to be pretty; she just has to be sea-worthy. And after three days in a storm, I have a whole new definition of what that means. Let's get some of the water out of the bilge."

Stone walked down into the cabin first. The inside looked as if a tornado tore up the inside. All the cabinets and the contents laid scattered about. There was water up over his ankles. Buck came down the gangway shaking his head back and forth.

"What a mess. Bet you wanted help during that storm. Somebody has a plan for you buddy, you better start believing, or he is gonna crap down your neck one day."

"It's all about perspective Buck. Something has a plan for me. Who knows what it is. So far, I have just been trying to stay alive. That has been enough of a challenge so far. I'll worry about plans later."

"Nothing for nothing Stone, but you just laid the biggest news of humanities existence on me, and you brought me here to help clean up your boat?"

"Not at all Buck, there's beer on shore, go have a few. I just wanted to get the *Spiritus* off the rocks before the damage got worse."

"Man you are one screwed up chicken-plucker Stone. You will never need a boat, a plane, a car, or even a bike again. Damn it man, you can fly a thousand times faster than the speed of sound. Do you get that? You're wasting time with this."

"Buck, have I ever left a friend behind?"

"Say no more, forget what I said, how can I help?"

"Besides, I don't even know if I will be alive in a few days, a month, or a year. I have no idea what has happened to me."

Stone opened the door to the engine room and walked inside. He cleared away all the floating debris.

"Can we use any of the batteries Buck?"

"Naw, they leaked all their acid out. Sea Water has gotten inside of them."

Stone leaned over the generator and pulled the oil dipstick out. It was clean and free of any signs of water. He then took a hand crank out of the tool cabinet. He turned on the starter switch, and pulled the choke out, just a little. He fitted the crank to the front pulley and began to rotate the engine; slow at first, then faster until the diesel engine began to sputter to life. They had power...at least for the moment.

He then rigged the battery switch so that electrical energy supplied to the inverter/charger was able to energize the main engine. After making sure the main engine was free of seawater, Stone went up to the cockpit, turned on the key, and pushed the starter button. The engine roared to life like there was no problem at all. That was a big relief.

Stone went back into the engine room and pulled the lever that engaged the emergency, engine driven, sump pump to start shipping water out of the boat. It did not take long to suck the keel sump dry. Every few minutes, Stone had to disengage the pump so more water could flow in. This went on for half-an-hour before all the water in the *Spiritus* was where it belonged: back in the sea.

Buck was trying to carry the bulky items to shore which provided much needed working space in the *Spiritus*.

"Wait a minute Buck, I have an idea. Just make big piles of stuff. I will take them to shore."

"Now that's an idea worth seeing happen."

Stone kicked a few items around like canned goods, clothing, and galley supplies forming a pile. He then leaned down, put his arms around the pile, and jumped to the shoreline.

Buck declared, "That has got to be the coolest talent I have ever witnessed."

Buck went about making piles, and Stone would transport them to the shore. It took another half-hour before the inside of the *Spiritus* appeared of junk and ready for the wet vacuum, which would suck up the residual water.

Stone was able to get the inverter working that supplied the 12-volt fans, spaced throughout the boat. They began to get the air circulating. He was also able to get the refrigeration and air conditioning working. All primary systems were operational except for the radio and navigational electronics. He could live with that. His new satellite phone and computer will work outside of the cave, and those will be all he needs.

Buck inspected the bilge once more and it was still dry. "Stone looks like the keel and the bottom are intact. There doesn't appear to be any leaks."

Stone replied, "How lucky is that? Ok, let's get back to my home office and see who we can trust to help figure out what this 'superpower' is all about. Buck, give me your arm."

"Wait, don't forget the beer."

"Yea...check that, let's get a beer, and then follow-me. I want to introduce you to someone."

Stone lead Buck to the smaller cave where Evens laid resting. "Buck, if this thing didn't happen to me I could have been that guy. He has been lying there over 342 years waiting for someone to find him."

"That's the Royal Navy? There is no record of them being in this area during that time. Is there?"

"The Navy was still young back then, and history is a funny thing. There are pigs on the island. That is evidence in support of ships anchoring here in the distant past. I just thought this was something you would want to know about."

"I did thanks. Should we bury him?"

"I don't know. Perhaps we should call the Royal Navy and let them know what we found. Just now, however, I am not ready to give up this island's privacy. We have time to think about it. Ready?"

"Five-by-five."

Stone took Bucks arm, jumped to where the case of beer was lying, and then jumped back to his office.

"If that doesn't get you dizzy Buck, nothing will."

"Roger that Flash Gordon."

Nothing is absolute; therefore, nothing can be an absolute truth. More so, all of knowledge is incomplete without the perspective of something else. The dogma of religions, even the teachings of the Buddha are not absolute: they remain only suggestions of a greater perhaps unknowable, ineffable truth.

6

LOOKING FOR ANSWERS TO IMPOSSIBLE QUESTIONS

Back at the apartment, Buck said only one thing, "Janet." Stone wanted to call her but did not want to lose time by having to explain too much. He might also sound harsh to someone that had been worried for a few weeks about his well-being. There would be answers to questions he needed to consider. He could not let just anyone know about these new abilities, not even Janet. He did not even know if he would be alive in a few days, much less in a few weeks. He called her from his new satellite phone. Her voice mail picked-up.

"This is Janet, you know what to do."

"Janet, I am alright. I was in a storm and there was damage to the boat. I am ok. Everything is ok. I'll be back in a few days. Call this number if you are having any problems I can help with. Other than that, again, do not worry, I am fine. There are some amazing stories we can share."

After Stone was finished with his call to Janet, he walked over and got two beers; he turned and gave one to Buck.

"Ok, we have two areas of inquiry. The first is what happened during that meteor impact? The next question is to which chemicals was I exposed.

"Next we need a very specialized and trust worthy doctor, a radiobiologist, to determine if the radiation poisoning I experienced is gone, or if there is damage to worry about.

"Then we need to organize a study to determine how this ability works, how it was formed, can it be duplicated?"

"If it can be duplicated, Stone, I would really like to be the first test subject."

"We need to be careful with this information, Buck. In the wrong hands, it could screw up entire civilizations. Can you imagine a Bin Laden, or even a Dick Cheney being able to jump around, moving things with impunity? Things like nuclear arsenals for god's sake!"

"Stone, there will always be terrorists."

"Sure, as long as there are Cheney's."

"Rodger that. Why do you think this happened to you?"

"Don't get all misty on me Cinderella. It was a freak accident. A meteor fell and exploded on a volcanic island. That is all there is. Some minerals got in the way."

"Yea, but just days before a freak storm blew you to the shores of that volcanic island against your will. What is that all about? Two freak events in a row that ends up with you having abilities—powers—that no human has ever displayed before."

"Something happened. I got sick. I really thought I was going to die. I was prepared to kill myself, but instead, I kept passing out.

Then I got stronger. I got hungry, I thought about Alfredo's and there I was. I don't know if this is a gift, a curse, an accident, or some short of a blessing. Buck, all I know for sure, there was a lot of pain and stress before I could jump. Moreover, there was a hundred times over a week's time span I should have died, but I did not. I want to let the science figure this out, and let us keep the idea of a plan, or a blessing in our hip pocket. There is an explanation."

"Ok then, who do we call to help figure this out?"

"You got any ideas? I think Bob from Miami can do the geologic work up and figure out the soil chemistry. He can probably get others to do some analysis on plants, water, and any dead animal remains that are still there."

"I know an astrophysicist from Penn State that is an expert in nuclear synthesis. Her name is Barbara."

"Theee...Barbara?"

"Yea...that Barbara."

"Then here is what we should do Buck. Let's ask them for a fee agreement to expedite a trip to the Virgin Islands, then have both of them sign non-disclosures. Give them the impression this is a top-secret expedition sponsored by the government. Then book them tickets to fly there. Rent a jeep. Drive them into the mountains where the vegetation is beginning to become very dense. Stop the jeep and have them put on hoods. Start driving them off road; make it very bumpy and disorienting. I will be waiting to jump in, and then jump the jeep and us to the project site in the Pacific. We will then walk to the camp. Before they get to the Virgin Islands, I will jump their equipment to the test area. They must not have any sort of global positioning equipment, cell phones, or cameras with them. They should bring enough supplies for three days of field work."

"OK, Stone, that takes care of what happened on the island. What are you going to do about getting yourself checked out?"

"I will find a doctor that specializes in radiation poisoning, and get checked out under a false name."

"We have a plan, let's get started."

Bob and Stone both went to graduate school at the University of Miami. Bobby stayed in research; Stone went into consulting. Bobby was a geochemist that studied the chemistry of the water found in pores of sediments in which seagrass and mangrove were growing. Especially in those areas found around the Turkey Point Nuclear Power plant, south of Miami, along the shoreline of Biscayne Bay. This was also the only area in the world where a thriving population of the endangered American Crocodile existed.

Stone called Bob.

"Geochemistry lab, this is Bob."

"Bob this is Stone, I know, I still owe you $20 dollars from the last poker game, but listen; you name your price, I need you on a plane with testing equipment by tomorrow afternoon. I want to meet you in St. Thomas at 7pm. You will be gone for three days. You have to sign a non-disclosure. You will wear a hood before arriving at the project site. It is on a tropical island and the project will be amazing. You will have help from an astrophysicist. I think she is pretty. No cell phones, no GPS, no cameras."

"Man you don't give a girl a lot of time to take a breath. What will I be looking for?"

"A meteor of unknown composition smashes into the side of an island volcano with large deposits of pitchblende. The surrounding rocks may have been involved and they contain biogenic carbonates. Steam vents were present at the time of impact with unknown mineral and metallic deposits. The steam is the only clue to recent underground conditions. There is significant evidence of recent uplift. All evidence indicates this is a basaltic volcano like the Hawaiian Islands, and not andesitic types like Mt. St. Helens. That is all the information I have.

"You will need to describe the geochemistry of the entire area and the vegetation as well. You will need a field lab. I can take care of the transportation. We also need a field generator."

"Stone that is really too short of notice."

"I will bring the twenty dollars with me, and enough Jim Beam to get us through the three days. There was a lot of lobster before the impact. Maybe they are still there. Buck will also be there."

"I wouldn't miss a change to drink with Buck for anything in the world. Who brings the Cubans?"

"Bob, I'll make sure there are a few boxes of fresh Cubans for the camp fire."

"Count me in. When do I leave?"

Things were a little rockier between Barbara and Buck. They use to date before he unofficially retired from the Navy. One time too many, when Buck was supposed to meet Barbara for dinner and drinks, he did not show up. She was stood-up in a bar, left fending off drunks on her own. It was a chronic problem with Buck. It was his only problem, but a huge one. He was not reliable.

Barbara was a beautiful sun-bronzed bombshell of a woman with long jet-black hair. Her eyes looked like bright mesmerizing gems of jade. The whole package was there; exotic looks, talent, smarts, and she was ambitious. She was passionate about her work, her life, and any love she cautiously entered into—something she never did easily, or without a lot of forethought. Therefore, when she finally resolved to love someone, it was purposeful. She fell in love for well thought-out reasons that matched the goals she had set out for her life—never because of ephemeral emotions: those were only there to wake-up a libido; or perhaps to alert a person that some other fit for their life was imminent. She never liked to fail when she settled on a goal, and liked it less because some jerk did not have his act together: especially, when she invited him into her world.

She would, if convinced of a potential worthwhile future, indulge in some frivolous sex with a potential candidate: just to see if the stud had what it took to sire a good bloodline: but also whether "it" had the endurance to keep momma happy. In her experience, a good buyer will always ride a horse before fully opening the wallet.

From her point of view, Buck was good horseflesh: rugged with good looks; strong, he could effortlessly toss her about in bed with one gentle hand, just as if she was a mere sack of potatoes. He was steamy and determined when aroused; unassumingly smart; brilliant in so many worldly matters; and he was kind. He was generous; money was only a tool for him, not his life. He was not materialistic, and never considered hanging with those that were.

A purpose drove Buck that he never openly discussed. He was mysterious; a simple soldier in the Navy, he would say. Buck was such a stud he even turned the heads of men when he made appearances in his dress whites, his choker full of metals. Some would even say his reputation alone would fill the room with anticipation, like trumpets sounding, minutes before he even entered. In his small clandestine circle, he was a legend. Buck was electrifying, and she loved him for it.

Barbara, of course, helped to turn heads a few times at military dinner outs, by wearing a revealing tightly fitted, very short white dress that significantly magnified her voluptuous curves. No woman appreciates upstaging antics that diminishes her spotlight, even unintended ones generated by her man. Once in retaliation, she pinned one of Buck's metals above her large left braless breast that always seemed to have an attention-drawing nipple poking out from behind the cloth. She would tell inquirers the metal was for naughty valor, way above the call of duty.

Once an Admiral stopped by to admire her metal, then he glanced at where it should have been on Bucks blouse. "Colonel, you seem to be out of uniform."

Buck would grin and reply, "Looking forward to it very soon sir."

To her, Buck looked even better undressed. He was dark and muscled, although covered with scars that she knew were once bullet holes, knife wounds, and gaping holes caused from compound fractures. Buck would call them old football or rugby injuries. She knew better. Buck would not talk about the scars and usually changed the subject by moving one large calloused hand down cupping both of her rounded hard cheeks, lifting her feet off the ground. Long ago, she gave up trying to stop him: when he made up his mind, there was no changing it: but his lust would certainly change the subject.

She was a part time surgical nurse while doing her doctorial work in stellar nuclear physics and the origins of matter at MIT. She wasn't dumb, there was no way a desk jockey, as Buck claimed to be, received so many purple hearts, bronze stars, silver stars, and one of the few medals of valor awarded a living soldier. She heard rumors at some of the parties that he had citations and metals locked away in secure vaults that no one, except a very special few, would ever know about.

Buck could never be a cad: he would never treat anyone like that on purpose: especially someone he could finally feel something for and trust. It was solely because he would get a phone call and only had minutes to jump on a helicopter destined for places unknown, possibly to kill people he would never meet; or to cross borders to gather critical information that could help high-level decision makers avert an international disaster. More than a few times, it was Buck and his team that stood between a decision to launch a nuclear attack or not. Sometimes a difficult decision prevailed to take the lives of a few nefarious leaders at the cost of a little travel expense, and a few bullets: it was better than risking the lives and wellbeing of hundreds of thousands of otherwise innocent people.

It was when the missions benefitted the bottom line on private corporate spreadsheets, and not the American people, for whom he swore to protect that he ran afoul with the administration. One-time too many, these atrocities happened, and lead to his unofficial retirement. He would always be there for the American people and for that matter, the entirety of humanity. It sickened him, nevertheless, when any elected official abused the power of a government office to line their pockets; or used government resources to improve private corporation's balance sheets. These politicians were too slick to take cash directly from the corporate representatives they helped. Instead, they would use the insider information created from the laws and rules they created, to buy stocks that rose or fell because of their actions. It was all too much for Buck to swallow.

Unfortunately, it was the downside of his job that he could not reveal his position as a navy seal in a special unit. He was on call 24/7, continuously at the Presidents beckon call.

Protocols did not allow him to cancel meetings or make other arrangements. When he got the call, he immediately had to go dark. It was a matter of security. High tech devices allowed spies to tap phones or monitor team members remotely: a change in routine would alert a spy to a team's mobilization. It did not take a rocket scientist to match a hot spot with the activation of a covert team. Premature disclosure could endanger the lives of everyone.

He could not even trust the intelligence agencies, much less the petty members of congress. Everyone had their alternative motives: it was not out of the ordinary for even trusted people within the government to give information to enemy combatants. Alternative agendas were always a threat, especially from those seeking media attention, power, or greater financial gain. Buck simply had to look like a cad.

Because of those facts, and after the last time Barbara was stood-up, without further discussion or ceremony, she simply stopped taking his calls over six years ago.

"What the hell do you want, dirt-bag?"

"Hi, Barbara, nice to hear your voice. How you doing?"

"Better, after you hang the phone up."

"You cannot be that mad at me, you still have my private number on your caller ID. Otherwise, how did you know it was me calling?"

"Go jump off a cliff, and leave me alone."

"Can't do it babe; I have a job for you. Except for cutting my jewels off, you name the price. There are a few rules, however, and now it's your turn to not only keep secrets, but also be part of them."

Buck went on to describe the same details Stone just finished describing to Bob.

Perhaps it was the intrigue, but more than likely it was the intellectual challenge that caused Barbara to say yes; agreeing to the scientific excursion to a remote island paradise with clear water and white sandy beaches: not to mention, being with that no good, arrogant, undependable Buck for three nights and days. Yea, that's right, it was the science.

As scheduled, Bob, Barbara, and Buck all met at the front of the St. Thomas airport. Buck was waiting for them in a hunter green and tan, four-wheel drive Jeep Cherokee.

After hugs between old friends, and introductions to potential new ones, and a slap from Barbara to Bucks face just to set the mood, Bob asked, "Where's the equipment?"

"Stone has a special delivery service." Buck replied, "They are extraordinary. I wouldn't be surprised if most of the equipment is already set up and ready for you to work on right now. Climb aboard. We need to meet Stone at seven sharp."

Indeed, earlier that morning, Stone jumped to the University shipping department and picked up Bob's crates in a rented U-Haul truck. When it was loaded, he drove to and parked the truck at a nearby Wal-Mart. He went inside the container area and touched the equipment as he thought about the old campsite near the pond: when he jumped there, nothing much had changed. Most of the rotten bananas were eaten, and so were the pieces of coconut left for "Mr. No Claws." The most obvious changes he noticed since the meteor impact was that the waterfall had started flowing again and he saw green returning to the tops of the palms and under-brush. He marveled at the dexterity of nature and its ability to rap-idly adapt and change. That is not something that happens over a few life times. It takes millions upon millions of years of learning and developing a method to pass those lessons up, to build another higher level of complexity.

After his short moment of admiration, Stone then jumped to the shipping department at Penn State.

There, Stone also elected to rent a U-Haul and do the same maneuver with Barbara's equipment.

Back at the island, Stone opened the crates. After he stretched the sail canvas and tied them to the trees, he took the equipment out and set it up on folding tables he brought from his home. The makeshift canopies will protect the sensitive equipment from the afternoon rains and the sun.

Stone dragged the generator out and put it next to the pond away from the tables. He unrolled an electrical extension cable and put the plugs next to the equipment. He used the jugs of diesel that he had previously taken from the *Spiritus* to fill the generator tank. With a quick pull on the crank, the generator fired up. They were ready. It was nearly 7pm in St. Thomas. Stone jumped to the place both he and Buck agreed to meet, after finding it on Google Earth.

Stone was standing next to the road when Buck and the crew came driving up.

"It is nice to see you again Bob, here is your $20: even nicer to see you Barbara. Buck has talked a lot about you. Sorry we have never met before. But I understand why Buck would want to keep you under wraps."

Buck whispered out of the side of his mouth, "Cool it, thin ice here."

Barbara replied, "Nice to know Buck even remembered my name. Where's the project site."

Buck took charge, "Ok, here is where you have to put on the hoods."

Bob asked, "Why the precautions? We already signed non-disclosures."

"Those are only to help put you in jail if you discuss this pro-ject with anyone. The hoods will help us stay friends and to keep the information as limited as possible."

With the hoods donned, Buck put the Jeep in gear and they started to travel off road for about a mile. That was when Stone jumped the entire jeep and its passengers to the pacific island on the other side of the world over 6000 miles away.

They landed in a small clearing and Buck abruptly hit the brakes. When they stopped Stone said, "Ok, we walk from here."

Buck just shook his head, "Now that was different."

The entire crew started to walk down a pathway towards the base camp. It took about thirty minutes. As they got close, Stone told Bob and Barbara they could take their hoods off. They were on the white pebble beach with the ocean on their left and the volcano on their right. The time of day was roughly the same just 24 hours ahead in the next day.

Stone had the base-camp set up, complete with hammocks, coolers full of food, some music, bottles of wine, beer, and everyone's favorite Jim Beam. There were also some very, very fresh boxes of unopened Cuban cigars, acquired only a few hours ago from a small village in Cuba, still wrapped in Grandma; Cuba's only official newspaper.

All the equipment was set up, calibrated and operational.

Stone had already built a nice fire and had some steaks on a grill, with seafood and fruits cooking in banana leaves he found earlier, away from the blast zone.

"Not bad for roughing it," exclaimed Barbara. "What are you guys going to eat and drink?"

She walked over, poured a neat class of Jim Beam, and opened a box of cigars. She picked out a long thick cigar and started to moisten the outside by sliding her wet tongue up and down the edges of the tobacco, she then bit off the end of the robust smelling stogy and spit it out over to the side. She glanced over at the boys and smiled. Then she walked over to the fire and bent over, deliberately showing off her perfectly round backside to the boys she knew would be gawking in wanderlust; she then picked up a burning stick to light the Cohiba.

The display was so sexy; such confusing blends of masculine and feminine strut; the guys began to squirm about, adjusting their belt buckles, and unconsciously shaking their heads back and forth. There was no question, this vixen was not only the master of the stars, but she also knew how to toy with the passion in men's hearts here, back on Earth.

Bob was the first to speak, "You know in Sweden one of those son's-a-bitches cost as much as $98.00 USD each?"

Buck dreamily said, "All day long..."

Bob spoke again, "How in the world can a woman be so masculine and yet still so desirable? That is so confusing it hurts."

"Put it back in your pants guys," said Stone, breaking up the illusion anyone but Buck had a chance at that prize, "We have work to do."

"Stone all these dead trees; a result of the impact?" asked Bob.

"Yea, I was here in the middle of the whole thing."

"What the heck?" Bob was exasperated, "There are no co-conut crabs in the Caribbean: only their smaller cousins."

Old Mr. No Claws and a few of his friends were lurking about in the trees above the camp.

Stone took charge, "Bob, Barbara both of you are going to see a lot of things that do not make sense in this area. I am asking that you focus on your task to examine the vegetation, animals, substrates, and the water for whatever you can find. Ignore their juxtaposition on the Earth and to each other.

"Earlier today I used your Geiger counter Bob, and walked around. There are elevated levels of radiation but nothing danger-ous to us that I can determine. Let me know if you find something different."

"We go a long way back Stone, I'll trust you to keep me out of trouble."

"Thanks Bob."

"Hey everyone," Stone called out, "Tonight let's eat and drink, and enjoy the moment. In the morning, there is going to be a lot of climbing, digging, and a lot of other work. Profiter de la fete! (Enjoy the feast)"

"When did you start speaking French?" asked Bob.

Stone replied with one word after holding up his phone, "Google!"

Everyone laughed, while picking up plates and utensils, and then heading over to sit next to the fire to eat from the banquet. Bob grabbed a bottle of Beam; there was no need for a glass. Stone had trained his classmates as to why, years ago—now it was just habit. Barbara fell in line; she enjoyed being treated like one of the guys.

Stone opened the seafood wrapped in banana leaves and laid it open in front of the group to start picking through.

Buck used a fork to pick up the steaks and put them on everyone's plates. The amount of food and drink was obscene. The Beam passed from person to person until one bottle after another went dry.

A while after she stopped eating, Barbara stood up and walked to the shoreline.

Bob said, "I swear I will believe in a god if she just takes her clothing off."

Barbara undid her pant's buttons and pulled them down. She took off her top and started wading into the ocean.

"Praise all that is mighty, I am saved. I am born again!" yelled Bob. "There is a superpower. I am no longer an atheist."

"I don't know about you, but I think I also need a swim." Buck mused.

After standing up, he stripped down and started to walk towards his previous love.

Bob spoke, "Now that is simply selfish. How the heck is a guy like me supposed to take my pants off now?"

"Carefully," Stone replied, "Very carefully."

Stone also stood up, stripped down, and walked to the ocean. The sun was going down and the waves were beginning to subside. Bobby entered the water and Stone said, perhaps louder than necessary, "You know, it's around sunset that sea snakes are normally eaten by sharks."

"Thank goodness mine found a hiding place." Buck said softly.

Barbara began to giggle.

"I believe four isn't company Bob," said Stone, "Let's go get drunk in the pond and leave this debauchery alone."

Locked in a love grip, only death could pull Buck and Barbara apart. Both of them slowly turning and moving about in the ocean with the sky on fire in the background. Every color in the rainbow seemed to swirl around them as the dusk sky slowly filled with bright stars and the blur of the Milky Way. The rights and wrong of history diminished, only the two of them mattered at this moment.

Back at the base camp, Stone and Bob jumped into the freshwater pool. This was the pool Stone first remembered. It had returned for an unknown reason, except the obvious; water from the mountaintop again began to fall.

"Hey Bob," Stone yelled out, "Don't pee in the water I am taking a drink."

"Sorry about that, too late Stone, you should have mentioned that sooner."

Both had a fresh bottle of Beam and a Cuban. It was hard to believe this was primitive camping and they were working hard to discover new scientific truths. Every profession had its sacrifices; this was theirs.

"Stone, we are in St. Thomas. I know this because I flew here. It says St. Thomas on my ticket. St. Thomas is located at a latitude north of 18 degrees 19 minutes and 34 seconds. That would mean the constellation Crux—the southern cross—should be very low in the southern sky. Regardless, of those physical facts, there it is extremely high in the southern sky. Something is wrong. Coconut crabs, corals that look out of place, and now the skies are warping and moving constellations around. What's happening here?"

"You are a good observer Bob, always have been. Like I said before, keep your eye on the ball. Things, other than what we are supposed to be looking at will not make sense."

"Stone I don't know how you did it, but if I was the team leader here, I would say we are in the southern pacific ocean and head hunters are about to jump out of the bushes any second."

A few seconds later, Buck and Barbara walked up to the edge of the pond and asked if they could join the party.

"Speaking of head hunters; look who just walked up." Bob said, "Buck, please go get another bottle and a few Cubans. Barbara jump in, this will only take a second, I promise you won't feel a thing."

Barbara's calm reply was, "I have no doubt about any of that, and the cold water doesn't seem to be helping your game either."

The red-faced Bob just shut up and sat back down into the pool. Buck walked away chuckling.

Stone could swear the temperature of the water went up five degrees before she got waist deep in the pool. He thought to himself, he needed to see Janet as soon as possible.

The good times rolled on for a few more hours in their private swimming pool before everyone dried off and got into their hammocks. One, however, remained empty: Buck and Barbara decided to share the same hammock for the night.

After all the surveys are concluded, and death tears us from this reality, only one finding will govern: there is no separation between this world and a heaven.

7

SURVEY FINDINGS

The morning came too quickly and there was a full day of work ahead of the team. Barbara was in a very good mood and had breakfast cooking before the boys even woke up.

"Hey guys, wake-up. It is time to get to work. We're not getting paid to sleep all day; or, are we?"

"Yea, let's get to work." Stone replied. "Darn, my head didn't hurt this much after the meteor hit."

The guys jumped into the pool to wash off. After drying off, they put on their work clothes and hiking boots, then everyone walked towards the smell of breakfast. Barbara had cooked eggs with left over lobster meat and cut up some bananas and coconut. Most importantly, there was fresh brewed coffee.

The only thing Stone said was, "It is official. I am over coconut and bananas for at least the next week."

When breakfast was over Bob, Buck, and Stone set up the Plane Table and began to calibrate the Alidade so they could run a base line starting at the beach then up the mountainside. The first thing they wanted to do was to map the crater and then the environmental impacts they may find within the blast area. They would then take surface samples while mapping the sample location. Later they would drill down into the sand and rock to determine what happened to the rock strata below the surface. It would be a long three days but by the end of the testing, they should have a three dimensional diagram of the entire blast area, as well as, some indication of what happened. Barbara would run the tests and help to unravel the genesis of the samples taken. Everyone hoped to recover remnants of the meteorite.

While the survey continued with the rock sampling, Barbara walked around bagging samples of plants and animal remains. The tissues will reveal anything out of the ordinary.

"Buck and Bob, I am going to walk into the interior a bit to see how far the impacts reached. I may also climb the mountain to look down on the impact area. Buck I will be gone for most of the day."

"Ok, Stone, see you when you get back." Buck knew Stone's actual meaning; he was bugging out.

Stone turned and started to walk towards the Jeep. When he entered the vegetation line, out of site of the others, he jumped to the apartment. There he showered, took a few aspirins, and changed into business attire.

The day before, Stone made an appointment with a doctor in California. He arrived on time and for once, a doctor was prompt. Stone scheduled a complete head to toe MRI so that he would have a baseline of his current condition. Stone required that the doctor agree to a few things before the examination. First, only he and the doctor would have access to any testing results. There would be no other assistants or nurses in the examination room. Next, the doctor could not keep files, only Stone would be able to keep files and data. Stone agreed to sign a release for the doctor under his assumed name--Atom Strong--and the doctor would sign a non-disclosure that eerily looked like a government document.

The doctor was reluctant to accept "Mr. Strong" as a patient, but Stone assured him this was a cash transaction with no insurance agencies involved. The initial information provided by Stone, intrigued and fascinated the doctor: albeit, nothing from the study could leave the room. The doctor was familiar with working under such restrictions.

The doctor had an impressive background in treating radiation poisoning and graduated top of his class at Harvard Medical School. He worked for nine years doing research on patients subjected to radiation before going into private practice. Peers considered him an innovator in the field.

"Come in Mr. Strong."

"Thank you for seeing me on such short notice Doctor."

"Radiation poisoning isn't something you want to play around with. Let's do a quick check with the dosimeter."

Stone said, "Did that already; it looks like low levels of exposure."

"Yea...it does look like low levels now, but you certainly got a higher dose before; or, you would not have lost your hair. It seems to be coming back already, and that is a good sign. Tell me what happened."

"Short story, minding my own business standing next to a mountain side when a meteor hits it and sends a type of green gas into the air showering glowing dust all over me. It looked like I was under an ultraviolet light, and St. Elmo's fire was outlining everything within visible range. I passed out; I was sick to my stomach with heavy diarrhea for about four days, my hair started failing out within 48 hours and when it was over, I was very hungry and thirsty. That's about it."

"I would agree it sounds like a reaction to radiation poisoning. Did you take any iodine tablets or other medications?"

"Nothing, I just rode it out."

"That must have been amazing; to witness a nearby meteor impact and to survive."

"It was and I am experiencing a few side effects."

"Like what?"

"Doc, let's do this a little at a time. Can we do the MRI first and then talk some more?"

"Yes we can. Do you know what we should be looking for?"

"No idea except for internal injuries, organ damage, brain damage."

"Ok, change into the gown and I will go prepare the MRI."

Stone laid flat on the table as the doctor flipped the switch that slid Stone's entire body into the narrow imaging chamber. A few minutes later the background music that Stone was listening to, was drown out by a loud pounding sound. It took nearly thirty minutes but when the scan was completed, the Doctor was speechless.

"Mr. Strong, can you please remain still a while longer? We need to rescan your entire head."

"I am fine, go on."

Once again, the Doctor restarted the scan and then stopped at Stone's mid-chest.

The Doctor walked out from behind the lead glass screen and flipped the switch to bring Stone out.

"Mr. Strong, do you feel ok now: any headaches?"

"Except for the effects of too much of a good time last night, I feel fine."

"I have something to show you. I ran this twice to be sure."

What Stone saw was disturbing to say the least.

"The entire left hemisphere of my brain is glowing white. I can't see any of the folds or lobes. Could that be a malfunction of the machine?"

"Perhaps," said the Doctor, "But unlikely. The other hemisphere is perfectly clear and so is the rest of your body. There are no problems with the machine. That is a true picture of your brain. Let's go into the other lab and attach some electrodes. Then we can monitor your brain waves to look for abnormalities."

Stone took off his robe and put on his street clothing. As they walked into the other lab for more tests "Mr. Strong" began to ask some probing questions of the Doctor.

"Doc, you were in research for nine years. Where did you work?"

"Mostly, out of Las Alamos National Laboratory."

"What did you do there?"

"Classified."

"Doc, were you monitoring native Indians and the effects of nuclear fallout on them?"

"What caused you to guess something like that?"

"Because I know a spunky woman lawyer that just loves a good fight with the government. She sued them on behalf of the Navaho Nation for deliberately setting off an open-air nuclear device, knowing the fallout would rain down on the tribe. They were unwitting human test subjects, and the lawyer got retired government officials to admit when and why the test was done."

"Yes, I was doing the follow-up studies on those patients: I quit the program out of repugnance. I could not even dream of modern day Americans doing something like that to other Americans. Because of the lies the government continued to uphold in that same trial, I resigned."

"So you would agree, without question, that some technologies and information should never be put in the hands of government."

"I agree there are only a few types of very special people that should be given special information and technology that should only be used in the most extraordinary of situations."

"Doctor, in a few minutes you are going to be learning a few things that, so far, only two very trustworthy people know. Our common link is that we have no thirst for power or money. We believe everyone lives on this Earth for a common purpose. We have dedicated the remainder of our lives to that end: to get the message out that there is more to life than power and wealth."

"Mr. Strong, I have dedicated my life to science and to help my fellow humanity. I have money, but it sits in a bank, I have a very meager lifestyle because of the time I put into my work."

"I did a lot of research on you Doc and my spunky lawyer friend vouchers for your integrity. Seems there was an unidentified informant that helped her gather the information and medical records she needed to make her case.

"Doctor, my name is Richards; Stone Richards. And before we go hooking up electrodes to my head, what is the one place you have always wanted to go, but never had the time to travel?"

"I always wanted to see Amsterdam."

Stone reached out and put his hand on the Doctor's shoulder. In a flash, they were in Stone's favorite Amsterdam museum.

"Doctor this painting is called "Night Watch" by the Dutch Master Rembrandt. We are in the Rrjks museum in Amsterdam. I will bring you back here when we both are ready for a relaxing afternoon. I promise you will enjoy every moment."

Then Stone jumped with the Doctor to the famous Red Light District. The Doctor was just standing there with his mouth and eyes wide open; as if he was going to scream but choked it back.

"When you come to Amsterdam you simply have to see this place. You can window shop for any type of sexual flavor you desire. I have been here twice and both times ended up laughing my head off instead of getting off. Over there you can get a beer or even a joint if you care to take a few tokes."

The Doctor carefully turned his head to look at one of Amsterdam's famous "coffee houses." Stone then jumped to the train station.

"Every time I come here I cannot help but stop and buy some French fries with mayonnaise sauce. Two orders please."

The girl behind the kiosk counter did not notice them jumping in; or for that matter, notice them jumping back to the Doctor's office--after Stone paid for the food with American dollars.

"What the hell was that all about!" yelled the doctor.

"Eat the fries they are very memorable."

"What just happened?"

"After you calm down just a bit we can discuss that. It is one of the side effects. One minute I am looking for my gun to blow my head off to stop the pain: the next minute, I think about being somewhere, and I go to that place. It is like being Zorba the Greek. The only physical side affects so far is a temporary loss of hair and half my brain is a light bulb. The half by the way, mystics say connects us to the rest of the universe.

"Doc I have always had a theory that the right brain's only purpose was to filter out the vast amount of information the left side is capable of connecting to. What if the exposure damaged my brain and allowed it to reconnect synapses in such a way that the filter has been removed?"

"Mr. Strong, I don't know what to say."

"Please call me Stone. Let's hook-up the electrodes."

As the doctor went about pasting on the electrodes, both remained quiet, the doctor visibly shaken.

"Doc, you really should try those fries."

The doctor picked up a fry without looking at Stone and dipped it in the mayonnaise sauce. Then he flipped on the Electroencephalography (EEG) monitoring device and began to watch the monitor. The doctor just shook his head in disbelief. He reached for a book off the shelf.

"Stone, here is a picture of a normal brain wave pattern. That is yours. There is nothing to compare with your scan. Every person and perhaps everything is a type of transmitter and receiver: everything sends out and receives electromagnetic transmissions: but this is extraordinary. Look at this, no matter what level I set it at, there is extreme activity. You seem connected to every frequency level. This is going to take a lot of time to figure out so I can weed out the multiple variables."

"Doc, do you see any types of tissue damage?"

"Other than the fact that your brain is glowing brightly; I see no damage at all."

"Want to see where the meteor hit and talk with the other scientists testing the site? You got a few hours?"

"Yes, I do."

The doctor asked to go to his house first to change into field clothes. Afterwards they both went to Stone's house so he could change back to his field cloths. Then they jumped to the island. The doctor remained disoriented.

"Ok Doc, you have to calm down. These people do not know where they are, just as you do not. They think they are somewhere on St. Thomas. Do not let them in on my condition. They are testing the soils and plants to determine the genesis of the radioactive cloud. I am going to introduce you as Dr. Rick; I do not want them to know your real name. Ok?"

"I understand. Ok."

Both Stone and the Doctor walked out of the vegetation line and on to the beach. The others were hard at work. Barbara was at the testing table running samples, while Bob and Buck were still mapping and collecting more data points.

"Barbara this is Dr. Rick"

"I didn't know there was going to be more of us."

"I flew him in; it was a last minute decision: Rick specializes in radiation poisoning. I thought it might be helpful if he worked with you and was able to see firsthand what mixtures of elemental minerals and compounds came out of the explosion."

"Like you said Stone, basic Uranium 235, some thorium, and potassium-40 is all I can find, but at a higher, still non-lethal, concentration than normal background found in other areas."

"It would not be out of the normal, to have a high concentration of radioactive material in a dust cloud and then have that drift away and disperse over a wider area," mused Dr. Rick.

Stone queried, "It has been over a week, I wonder why the US Air Force or some other country has not dispatched a group here to see what this anomaly was all about. Surely, the satellites have picked up this radioactive signature and scared the hell out of them."

Dr. Rick said, "You said the cloud stayed only a few hours correct? Then perhaps they chased the signature after the cloud left and didn't bother to determine its origins."

"Nonetheless, Stone, I am prepared to give you my preliminary analysis," said Barbara. "There is nothing extraordinary here; only the above normal levels that would be consistent with a meteor impact that disturbed a concentrated ore deposit. The trees were damaged by heat and they are now recovering."

Stone asked, "What about the dead fish?"

"A nagging mystery so far; I found some very rotten samples but like everything else, nothing out of the ordinary. Perhaps the shock wave killed them; like tossing dynamite in the water."

"Thanks Barbara, I am going to take the Doc back to town. Tell the boys I am going to stay in town tonight and drive back in the morning. You should still have everything you need."

"We are fine, but I think we can save you some money and get out of here tomorrow. We will know more later-on as we start to synthesize all the information tonight."

With that, the Doctor and Stone turned and walked back into the vegetation line. Stone put his hand on the Doctors shoulder and thought about the Doctors office.

"So what do you think Doc?"

"So far I am flabbergasted. I have no idea what is going on, but I will continue to work on it. When can you come and see me again?"

"I can be here in the morning."

"Ok, I will have a few tests designed. I am going to cancel all my appointments and keep the staff away tomorrow."

"What do I owe you for today?"

"Stone I am wondering if I shouldn't be paying you for this opportunity. This is amazing. I will see you tomorrow."

Stone had another important meeting. He jumped back to his home, took a shower, and shaved the stubble from his face; then he shaved around his ears and squared off the stubble on the back of his neck. He had not looked like this since the first day of boot camp. After putting on cologne, he jumped to the front of a door on the sixth floor in a Cape Canaveral condominium that faced the Atlantic Ocean. He knocked on the door.

When the door opened, Janet shrieked, "Stone! Are you ok? I missed you. Where have you been? Look at you. Look at your hair... Where is your beard? Come in!"

Janet pulled Stone, into her condominium, and then would not let him go. The last time they saw each other she was boarding an airplane destined for the USA to receive a medical treatment. Apparently, she got some kind of a bug or parasite from eating raw fish in Chile: The medics did not have the medicines she needed in the Galapagos Islands.

Stone's first thought was to jump her right into the bed; but instead, he took the more conservative route of taking her hand and walking her into the bedroom where he slowly began to re-move her clothing as Luis Miguel crooned in the back ground.

It was a slow and deliberate reunion: gentle and at the same time intense. The passion persisted well into the night. Afterward, they were both spent and drifted into a deep sleep that lasted late into the morning. He had no answers to her questions, only a burn-ing desire to be with her. For the moment that was all she needed.

What would it be like to be a photon: an elemental particle without mass, or a charge, neutral in every sense of the word? If you were the master of photons, like them, you would be able to move at the speed of light. There would be no concept of space, time, or gravity, just vast amounts of energy swirling all around you. Without the photon, there would only be declining enthalpy. With the photon, however, complexity continues to build. The environment around you would bend to your will.

8

LIFE BEGINS IN PHASES

In the morning, Stone got up to make breakfast for Janet. The sun was shining over the Atlantic Ocean. The sunrise framed by the balcony sliding doors also allowed a sea breeze to flow into the living room.

Janet still had questions, but he could not answer all of them. He explained the shipwreck and partially, the hair loss: the style now looks like a very close buzz cut. She was a very smart woman: he had to be careful about any lies. In fact, he avoided having to makeup a lie. He preferred to ask her not to ask questions and just be happy he was home. When the time was right, he would talk more about it. For the moment that was fine for her. She had other worries to fret over, now that she knew he was ok.

Stone sensed that there was something askew. He put it aside thinking it was because of his aloofness concerning the shipwreck and his hair loss.

After breakfast, he jumped back to the Doctors office. Tests were set up to help them both understand what was happening.

"Stone," the Doctor started. He stood up from his leather chair situated behind an old mahogany desk made of wood salvaged from a sunken Spanish sailing vessel. At least that is what he paid an exorbitant price to own. "I watched a video on TED.com; amazingly, inventors devised a headset that read the alpha brainwaves passing over the scalp. With the headset's help, software took the information transmitted wirelessly from the persons brain and translated it into computer speak, which allowed the computer to do what the person was thinking about.

"At this moment it is just making a cube turnaround, shrink, or disappear. But that's just a very tiny step into a much larger possibility: imagine being able to train your brain with this feedback to do things humans have been day dreaming about for millenniums. Like any muscle, brains must exercise and be trained to learn higher functions. The headset will make it easier to break existing thresholds. Nonetheless, your brain demonstrates the next step into an endless universe of possibilities.

"Here is one of my theories; anybody can do virtually anything they want to do; that is if they can control their concentration. We are all made of energy: the exact same stuff atoms are made of--elemental particles. Everything is immutably connected. Moreover, energy is simply frequencies. For a radio station or a television, all you have to do is dial in the channel you want to listen to or watch: filters remove all the unwanted frequencies and static. Humans dial in by concentrating. Controlling our concentration allows us to filter out the static, which distracts us from seeing or doing what we really want in our lives.

"I theorize that whatever modifications were made to your brain during the meteor impact, now allows you to concentrate and control frequencies. The glow we see in the MRI may result from a higher energy level that allows you to select much smaller frequencies that normal humans or even machines cannot detect.

"I am calling what you do, phasing in and out from one state of matter to another: selecting the channel or level of the electromagnetic spectrum you want to exist in.

"It doesn't appear you change the matter that surrounds you: more so, you simply become a form of energy--a frequency--that allows you to pass through solid matter until you decide to stop and shift phases back to the solid phase we now exist in.

"The images you think of for your destinations are simple road maps. When you travel at the speed of light there is no time for thinking, the subconscious brain does that for you as it does for your heart beat, breathing, healing a wound, or growing hair or fingernails. Electromagnetic radiation moves at the speed of light and passes through anything--so do you!

"There may be many other things you can do that you are currently not aware of. I have devised a few tests to verify my thoughts and to help you understand these new abilities.

"Everything should follow Einstein's laws of relativity. There is no since starting out from an unknown point. Let's start by measuring from known points. Put this monitor on, if I am correct it cannot monitor you during a phase walking event, you should be moving too fast for it to record. If you visually monitor it, however, during a phase walk, you would be able to see it record and even see the results: but that data would only be relative from that perspective: back at this perspective, or reality, the data should only look like a dot or a straight line for some short duration.

"In this reality, we should see the activity unique to your brain; when you phase walk the activity should look like you stopped transmitting or receiving signals.

"So again, put the electrodes on and go as far as you can. If you can think about circling the Earth, 50 times or more, without shifting back do so. The idea is to stay in the phase walking mode for as long as possible. Also, keep your eyes on the monitor. Remember what you observe."

Without further question, Stone proceeded. He simply thought about a journey without a destination and the room became total whiteness, nothing had form, it was all energy. There was no up; no down; there was no gravity. There was no sense of movement. Stone looked at the monitor and indeed, it was operating normally, his brain was in an elevated state of activity in this phase, the same as in the solid phase. When Stone decided to phase shift back no one was there.

After a few seconds, the Doctor reentered the room.

"There you are. I said a few times around the world, not the universe. Where did you go?"

Stone looked confused. "I only phased walked for a few seconds."

"Stone it has been four hours. I really started to worry about you. That is amazing, I am four hours older, and you are four hours younger as measured by our relative times. That blows my mind. You could possibly stay in that space for a few months and everyone else you knew, would all be old or dead. Nothing would be the same for you. What did you do: what did it look like?"

"There was total whiteness; except for a few hues of blue or red. There was no sense of movement. There was no sense of space or perspective. It all seemed neutral. The monitor worked as you predicted. I could see the monitor work like it did in this office."

"Let's see the monitor."

Stone turned it to show him. There it was, proof. The recorder showed his normal level of activity, before he phased walked, then a straight line representing a few seconds of time, and then his normal brain activity started again.

"My guess would be, if we could see or measure at the same quantum levels that elemental particles exist, the patterns for your brain activity here, where there appears to be none, would match exactly the activity on either side—Amazing!"

"Doc?"

"Yes, of course, this remains between us. I understand the potential ramifications completely."

"Doc there was a time on the island when I was able to put my hand inside of a tree and pull out some heart of palm."

"Really, leave the monitor on, try to put your hand in the cabinet and pull something out."

Stone stood up and turned around. At eye-level, there was a wooden cabinet. He tried to put his hand inside, but his hand stopped as it reached the surface.

"Interesting," said the Doc, "Try getting some pills out of the glass cabinet over there."

Stone walked to the glass cabinet. With ease, he slid his hand through the glass and pulled out a bottle of pills.

"Ok, come back over here, and look inside the cabinet."

Stone walked back over and opened the cabinet. He could see a box of rubber gloves, some trays, and some bottles of alcohol.

"Close the door and now think about what you want to take out."

Stone thought about the box of gloves and then reached for them. His hand easily slide into the wood cabinet and returned with the box of gloves, all without having to open the cabinet.

"Brilliant," exclaimed the Doctor, "You have to know what you want before you can use your ability to phase shift. It makes sense, Stone? Why use valuable energy and resources to wander around not knowing what you really want? First, stop, think about what you really want, and then go get it. That explains why some people are more successful than others are. Successful people have determined what they want and then concentrate on getting that and nothing else. I think there is a lot more going on here than meets the eye Stone."

"Like what?"

"Don't know yet, but be ready for an amazing ride."

"What about the flash light in my brain Doc?"

"Let's draw some blood to see what is in it."

Stone rolled up his sleeve, as the doctor pulled out a tray full of "forks and knifes" for sampling blood.

The Doctor tied off the upper part of Stones arm with a rubber strap. When he tried to insert a needle, however, it passed thru the skin, hitting nothing solid. The doctor could move the needle about within the skin just as if it were a glass of water.

Faking a thick Texas accent the Doctor exclaimed in surprise, "That just ain't right!"

Stone nodded his head and said, "Here we go again."

"Don't get excited, I have a few ideas."

The doctor picked up a scalpel and tried to make an incision into Stone's arm. He could not do it. It passed through the skin just like the needle.

The doctor used his hand to touch Stone and the arm felt solid. The doctor thought for a second and then thrust the scalpel into Stone's chest. The scalpel and the doctor's hand went through Stone as if it were air. Stone did not feel a thing.

The doctor turned away and the turned quickly trying to slap Stone in the face. Nothing connected. The doctor seemed to be swinging at air.

"Looks like an unconscious self-defense mechanism."

"Doc you think bullets will just pass through me?"

"Want to find out?"

"Not really, let's wrap this up for now. I need to get back to the team. So what do you think? Any health issues or side effects I need to be aware of?"

"Stone I have no idea whatsoever. All we can do is keep monitoring you. We can do another MRI in a few weeks. But right now you won't even give me blood."

"Give me the needle Doc."

Stone stuck the needle into his own vein and drew out a vial of blood. He looked up at the doctor.

"Need anymore?"

"Amazing: no that will due for now."

"Stone what about everything else: physical contact with others for instance? Is everything working ok... there?"

"Interesting you asked, yea, everything is five-by-five, tested all that out last night."

All beings are manifestations of the original source. The most destructive illusion, from which humanity must be saved, is that individual existence is real.

9

EXTRAORDINARY BECOMING ORDINARY

Stone "Phased Walked" back to his home and changed into his clothing for the field. He was feeling better now that he had an idea of the physics behind his ability. He began to think of the vegetation line next to the beach.

Stone walked out to the beach and then up to the camp. He stopped for a minute and decided to return. When he got back to the vegetation line he phase walked up to the top of the mountain. The image was spectacular: a 360-degree view of the Pacific Ocean, with a coral fringed volcanic island sitting in the middle of it. He walked over to a cliff and looked down to where the meteor struck. He used his phone to take a few pictures of the impact area. Using known distances on the ground, the team should be able to establish a relative scale for the image and get some more measurements.

Stone again thought about the clearing and was there. He laughed aloud because of this new level of productivity. What a tool.

Everyone was at the camp having a beer waiting for Stone.

"There he is our lost leader."

"Sorry Buck. Sorry guys that was an important meeting with the Doctor. Do you have any conclusions?

Barbara said, "My story remains the same: nothing out of the ordinary resulting from an extraordinary event."

"Same here," said Bob, "A big galactic rock smashes into the side of a volcano and temporarily messes things up before nature begins to repair the damage: the circle of life keeps going round and round. Whatever the meteor was comprised of, we may never know. There is no trace of it down to a hundred feet. That is all the drill piping I brought with me. We should have at least found fragments of the meteor in the crater fill deposits, or in the ejecta. We found nothing, however, except for some shock melt glass created by the extreme heat during impact. Why you are still alive is a mystery. The heat must have been very contained and directed in one specific direction."

Buck said, "We did find something interesting; an opening to a rather large cave. Want to see it?"

"Sure," replied Stone.

Everyone grabbed a beer and hiked past the oblong impact area, then up onto the mountainside to where a large opening was intermittently venting hot moist air: when the hot air reached the cooler pacific breeze, the moisture would condensate into a mist.

"Already checked for toxic gases, there are none," said Bob.

Stone crawled inside the hole until he found a cavern where they all could stand up. Like in the other cave where *Spiritus* was stored, areas on the cave's ceiling had fallen, creating skylights that lit up the interior. The cave looked like it had no bottom except where a huge river of molten lava was flowing over a thousand feet below. Stone could see where the level of the lava would occasionally rise and fall in the cave.

"This is spectacular. I have never seen anything like this before. It is a massive lava dome. It seems to have no end," said Stone. "Why are there no toxic gases coming out of this vent?"

"My guess," responded Bob, "Is that the nasty gases from the lava are flowing to the higher levels along that wall on the other side that is acting like a chimney. Here the cool air is drawn in and heated up. At varying times, backpressure causes the resulting hot air to blow out the cave opening—like a puffing dragon. Kind of makes you think about where the stories of fire breathing dragons came from, doesn't it?"

"Holy stolen tamale," Buck fumed, "It is hotter than a Billy goat in a pepper patch."

They all turned around to go outside. Upon exiting the cave, the view became breathtaking. The vista provided by the vast Pacific Ocean, the snow-white beach, and the tropical vegetation filled their souls with bewilderment.

"Is it any wonder primitive man felt the need to invent a god: what other way could ignorance describe such unimaginable beauty?" For a brief moment, Barbara was taken aback by the landscape.

"Ok guys," said Stone, "That's it. Here are some aerial views of the impact area. If there is nothing new, we are done."

"When did you get these?" asked Bob.

"Yesterday," replied Stone.

"I won't ask why the time stamp says just 20 minutes ago," Bob was still fishing, "It would take at least half a day to get back down from the top of this mountain."

Stone just thought what an idiot he was for not thinking about changing the time stamp before taking the picture--rookie mistake.

"Alright, let's get your stuff and I will have another crew pick the equipment up and deliver it back to your universities."

"Fine with me," said Bob, "I couldn't take another night of these bunnies humping in the hammock. All I heard, all night, was crabs and coconuts hitting the ground. I had to sleep with a helmet."

Barbara just smiled, as she looked Bob straight in the eyes and made sure her soft breasts brushed up against him as she passed by...slowly. Bob mused, "Where that woman stands is so hot, birds have to use oven mitts to pull worms out of the ground."

Barbara asked, "Ok Stone, can you tell us where we are now?"

"No way Barbara, I also need everyone's notes and test results before we leave."

After they gathered up their things and began the walk back towards the jeep, Stone asked Buck if he wanted to fly back with him. Buck sheepishly described the news that he and Barbara were spending a few more days together in St. Thomas, and that he would be flying back with her.

"Everything good with you and Doc Rick?" asked Buck.

"It's all good. We will talk later. Ok, everyone let's put the hoods on, the trips a lot faster on the way back, I promise you."

Stone and Buck walked the hooded pair through the jungle for five minutes before Stone phased walked them to jeep.

"Alright, here we are: be very careful," said Buck, "the jeep is just in front of you."

After everyone got in, Stone phase walked everyone to St. Thomas. Buck started the jeep and after ten more minutes of driving, the scientists took off their hoods.

"Buck, I am going to get off here. My jeep is just on the other side of that tree line. I may muck around here a bit. Barbara, it has been a very memorable pleasure, seeing all of you. Bob I owe you one. I may come by and see you in Miami in a few weeks. There will be a box of Cubans for you packed with the equipment."

After hugs and handshakes, everyone was done with their goodbyes, and Stone was free to go home and relax with Janet for the afternoon. Secure in the idea he was not going to die any moment.

Seconds after the research team was out of sight, he phased to his house, showered and shaved again, and changed his clothes. He then phase walked to Janet's front door. He knocked.

Janet answered. Her hair was a mess and she had been crying.

"Ok, girlfriend what's up? It is time to come clean. What is wrong?"

"Look who is asking questions, the mystery man himself."

"Barbara, tell me please."

"I'm scared. This morning the Doctor diagnosed me with breast cancer. It is at an advanced stage. I did not want to worry you until I knew for sure. That is why I had to come back and leave you in the Galapagos."

"What are the doctors saying they are going to do?"

"A full double mastectomy followed by chemo-therapy. I will have less hair than you do now."

"Honey, let's go see your doctor. I have to see the x-rays."

"Stone, what can you do? You are not a doctor."

"Honey...please." Stone may not be a doctor but he has learned a few things about himself that doctors could never imagine, much less be willing to discuss in public.

While Janet got ready, Stone picked up his phone and called Doc Rick in California.

"Doc you know anything about breast cancer and mastectomies?"

"Sure I do. Most cancers seemed to evolve from monkey viruses that most recently mutated during polio vaccination experiments in the early sixties; some cancers evolve through continual exposure to radiation that mutate DNA sequences. That is the core of my expertise."

"I need to see you in a few hours."

Stone and Janet drove to her doctor's office. The doctor was kind enough to see them for five minutes. They all walked into his office as the nurse brought in Janet's breast x-rays. The doctor put them on the light table.

"Here you go Mr. Richards, right there is the mass we are concerned with. We did a biopsy and found it to be malignant."

"Doctor, can you sketch me a picture of how the tumor is attached?"

"Why in the world would you want to know that?"

"Humor me Doctor I am a very curious type...Please."

"Well, most of the time a cancer cell starts when the DNA coding in a cell goes "haywire" mutating due to heredity or environmental causes; these cells grow out of control using up valuable resources needed for other organs. They can be benign staying in place, or become malignant and metastasize to other parts of the body through lymphatic fluids or the bloodstream. Cancerous cells are cells the body does not recognize as being part of your body.

Therefore, your body's immune system begins to attach them. Sometimes that is enough. If the immune system is overwhelmed and the cancer spreads untreated, the resulting tumors can be fatal. In all cases, the tumor is typically fed by blood vessels."

"When you cut out the tumors, what do you do with the blood vessels that feed them?"

"Most of the time, I do nothing. Sometimes I will clamp or tie them off with suture. Eventually they dry up absorbing back into the body."

"Janet here is the car key. I will meet you later at the condominium. I have a plan."

"Stone, where are you going?"

"Have I ever let you down?"

"No…"

"Doctor, I need those x-rays. I will return them in a few hours."

Stone took the x-rays before the doctor could object and walked quickly out the door. He looked around and saw that no one was watching. He phase walked to Doc Ricks office.

"Hey, Doc?" Stone called out.

"I am in the examination room!"

Stone walked into the examination room and hung Janet's X-ray on a backlit screen.

"Look Doc, there is a tumor. Why is that any different from a pill bottle in a medicine cabinet? Except for the fact it is attached to a human being."

"Your friend?"

"My love."

"Ok, what do you want to do?" asked the Doctor.

"Learn how the tumor is attached. Practice removing one from a cadaver, and then go get that monster out of her."

"How?"

"What if I can see down into the molecular structure of her breast? If so, an operation would be nothing more than trimming a mole or wart off the epidermis of someone's arm. My concern is how to stop blood flowing from the blood vessels that might be feeding the tumor. Why does removing a tumor have to be more complicated than reaching into a tree, or a cabinet to remove something?"

"Ok, let's go to the university hospital. I have a few friends there that could find us a cadaver with a tumor still inside."

Stone grabbed the Doc's arm and phase walked him to the hospital.

The Doc spent about an hour talking to attendants until they found what he was looking for: a middle-aged woman who died with untreatable malignant tumors in her breast.

"Stone come with me."

Both walked down the hall to the morgue where bodies donated for scientific research were stored.

"Ok, Doc, first I need detailed medical images of a breast with all the different tissues, lymph nodes, nerves, and blood vessels."

The Doctor found a medical book with the illustrations that Stone needed to see. Next, he described all the various parts and functions of the breast to Stone.

"Now come over here Stone. Look into her breast; can you see the details inside?"

Stone began to look but could only see epidermis. He put his hand inside her breast and felt a hard unevenly shaped lump.

"I have it, but I am afraid if I pull it out, I will tear open blood vessels or perhaps cause nerve damage on a living patient."

"You may be right. Just keep thinking about the inside of the breast. Ignore the epidermis. Think of a network of blood vessels and nerves with no tissue or muscle."

Stone removed his hand and stood back for a second. He started to see a person instead of a body and began to feel ashamed of his selfishness. He was so worried about Janet he passed over the contributions this woman had made with her life. The most important to him at this moment was the donation of her diseased body so that another could live. No one knows what their true purpose in life is, but because all life and non-life depends on each other's existence, everything always influences everything else. The entire universe is a house of cards, each one holding the other up.

Stone, in his own way, gave a silent prayer of thanks to an unknown woman who at the end of her life thought of the ones she was leaving behind.

Stone began to see what he needed. Everything around him turned to pure energy. Everything even the Doc was nothing more than outlines of energy with varying degrees of density.

Stone could see his fingers inside of the dead woman's breast holding the golf ball sized tumor.

"Doc, give me the surgical scissors please."

The Doctor handed them to Stone. Stone pulled gently on the tumor, moving it away from the other tissues. He could see where it was connected. It was mobile and only attached in an area about one half inch long. He saw where there was good tissue and the bad tissue. He began to cut the tumor away starting in the good tissue 3 millimeters away from the start of the bad tissue and the little veins he could also see protruding into the good tissue. It took less than 15 seconds. Stone pulled the detached tumor from the dead woman's breast.

Stone said, "If only it was that easy."

"It could be. Let's go take a look at it under the microscope."

The Doctor put the tumor under a dissecting scope and turned on the top mounted camera. An image projected on the wall in front of them.

"How did you know about the blood vessels coming out of the tumor? Looks like you got them all—amazing"

"I could see them Doc. Plain as day: a pattern that just did not seem to belong there."

"You called it right. Feel better?"

"Absolutely: Ok Doc, when I successfully remove the tumor, will Janet need chemo-therapy?"

"The interesting thing about this situation Stone, is that you can see if a tumor returns and you can take it out. Who knows what that means? Let's do this one step at a time. Take the tumor out and bring it to me."

Stone phase walked the Doc back to his office and then re-turned to Janet's condominium. He was cooking dinner when she walked in.

"How did you get here before I did?"

"I am on this hyper-efficiency kick, making the most out of every day. There are your x-rays. No worries."

"What the hell do you mean—no worries-are you mad? Or, are you just delusional?"

"Perhaps I am a little of both. Sit down please have a glass of wine. I made this paste out of herbs and spices you can spread on tomatoes, celery, or virtually any vegetable you want. I want you to eat as many organic raw vegetables as you can stomach for a while. This herbal paste has all the medicines your body will need. Right now let's eat, watch a movie, and forget about problems until the morning."

"Stone, if I didn't know you, I would think you are playing with me. For now I am too worried and tired to argue."

Stone and Janet enjoyed their meal and later watched a movie. Stone gave her a sleeping pill so she would not wake up during the procedure. Janet had no idea Stone was planning to remove her tumor.

When Janet fell asleep in his arms, still on the couch, he picked her up and carried her to the bed. He took her clothes off and then walked over to the counter where the surgical tools were stored that Doc had given him.

He walked back and leaned over her naked body. He began to concentrate. Slowly her body and all around him turned into outlines of varying intensities of energy. He could clearly see the mass her doctor had called a malignant tumor.

Stone picked up the scissors in one hand and began to palpate the tumor with the other. He moved it about and found it attached with the narrowest treads of tissue. Unlike the dead woman's tumor, this one showed no veins extending into the good tissue. He cut it off then pulled the malignancy out of her breast. The procedure was completed. He looked carefully under her armpits, between her thighs, around her neck, anywhere an infected lymph node might grow. There were no other abnormal masses of tissue found.

He could not help but stare in amazement as her heart continued to pump and her lungs contracted in and out. He could see blood flowing down into her legs and then back up towards her heart. He knew everything visible in the universe was solid, but then again he could see, for a fact, everything is just little pieces of differing forms of energy that emit unique frequencies that represent their individual forms. He could see both, solid and a pure energy phase, as no other human has. He could see it, but still knew, no matter how hard he tried, it was not meant for him to understand it; at least not in this lifetime.

It was true Stone was no Doctor, but his gift allowed him to see "white" energy and a "darker" energy: in other words, he could see a dark mass literally sucking good energy away from healthy tissue, causing the slow death of its host: the darkness was acting like a parasite would. It was no different from watching crime and corruption sucking the life out of a community. He was no doctor, but he knew what needed eradicating.

He sat down to reflect on the last few months. No person knows how their individual actions will affect the future of others. If Janet told Stone about her health suspicions, before she left the Galapagos, Stone would have insisted on escorting her back home. Instead, she kept her secret and Stone ended up where he was destined; to meet up with a meteor that changed his life. Life's truest conundrum is, if everyone choices the right path when they encounter forks in a road, looking back always appears as if life is preordained. He wondered what else would result from this confluence of events.

Stone put the tumor into a specimen jar. He washed his hands and walked back over to put covers on Janet's naked body. Before leaving, he leaned over and kissed Janet. He was thinking how fortunate his life had been and how much more fortunate it has become. It seemed now, he could not imagine a life without this woman with whom he had found love. Stone turned his attention to thinking about Doctor Rick's office.

"Here you go, just minutes after the procedure."

"Let's go take a look," said the Doc.

The Doctor stood up from his mahogany desk and began walking towards the examination room. After cutting the tumor open and making thin sections he looked at the samples under a high power microscope, the doctor said, "Congratulations Stone, it is not malignant. Her doctor was wrong."

"Wow that is great. Thanks."

"How is Janet?"

"Sleeping like a baby: now I need to figure out how to explain she has nothing to worry about anymore."

"Stone that should be the least of your problems."

In the morning, Janet and Stone woke up together. Janet rolled off her side of the bed and started to walk towards the bathroom. She stopped and turned.

"At least you could have put a t-shirt on me you pervert."

"I could have, but then the pictures would not have sold for as much."

She turned and started to walk away but not until she said, "You better use that money to take me out for dinner."

A few minutes after going to the bathroom, Janet came running out, still naked. In her low, husky, and excited voice she explained, "Stone the lump is gone. There isn't any lump, do you hear me: feel, there is no lump!"

"Yea...I do hear you," Stone was reading the morning news on his cell phone. "Maybe you should call the doctor and take his x-rays back to him. Have him do a few more tests."

"What the hell is going on Stone?"

"How in the world would I know? Go have some more tests. I need to meet Buck this afternoon. Now let's eat breakfast. Remember to eat a lot of that herbal paste."

Stone was feeling proud with himself. Not about lying: for helping to avoid a potential tragedy.

A pessimist sees difficulty in every opportunity; An Optimist sees the opportunity in every difficulty. Winston Churchill

10.

A FRIEND IN NEED

"This is Buck, speak."

"Buck when you get this message please give me a call. I am at the home office."

An hour went by before Buck returned Stone's call.

"What's up Master?"

"How was the vacation Buck?"

"Amazingly, I didn't have a clue a scientist could have such a short memory."

"Maybe she just likes your rotten *Gluteus maximus*."

"Maybe, it is fairly extraordinary...what's up?"

"If you have time, let's go to Alfredo's for lunch. I will catch you up."

"You coming to get me or do I take the traditional travel methods?"

"Take your car, I'm riding my bike. If I keep doing this phased walking I might end up forgetting what legs are for."

This time the front door bell rang as Stone walked into Alfredo's Paradiso. Immediately, however, Stone realized something was terribly wrong.

Alfredo was not his normal happy self. There was a problem. Stone could feel it in the air. Alfredo did not even turn from making a pizza to acknowledge Stone's arrival.

"Alfredo, can I have a large pepperoni with extra cheese?"

"Sure, sure soon it come."

"Alfredo, damn it, what is wrong: now tell me."

"Sassolino," Alfredo turned around, he obviously had not been sleeping, his face was drawn, and his eyes were red. "My father has been kidnapped. They want money but I know if I pay, they kill him anyway. My father taught me their ways when we were young. We knew this day comes. He told us, if it did come, we think of him as dead."

"That's crazy Alfredo, who has him. Do you have an idea of where he is at?"

"Somewhere in Palermo; that's all I know. I not been-a there in four years. I do not know his habits. But I know-a it's the Cosa Nostra in that area—the Mafia. Now they have him, they will kill him in revenge for all that he has done to them. It is their way."

"What did he do?"

"He is a poliziotto. He would not take bribes and would arrest anyone that offered him one. A week ago, he stormed into the estate of a Don and tried to arrest him and his capitani's for the murder of a local judge who also refused bribes. For this he will die. He has not been seen since."

"Who was the Don?"

"I don't know. I called his Commander. My father said to me once he can be trusted. His Commander said my father kept these things to himself so nobody would tip off the Mafioso about what he was doing. What can I do, but begin to be luttuoso—be mournful?"

"You can begin by being hopeful. What day is it?"

"It's-a Friday."

"Do me a favor Alfredo, when they call again, suggest to them, you will pay. Also, say you cannot get them the money until Tuesday or Wednesday because you have to sell some stocks and turn them into cash. Plead for them to spare your father's life, tell them you will bring him to Florida to live, far away from them. Tell them you must speak to him first to have proof of life. This is important; when they call, I must be on the phone to hear them. Have Linda answer the phone. Tell her to say you are not here and give them a time when you will return. Make sure I have enough time to get here."

"How much time you need Sassolino?"

"Seconds, just call me before you take the call."

"Alfredo, I have to go, do not take the call until I am here. Be hopeful my friend, I may have a few tricks I can pull off. If you don't mind, give me that pizza in the oven—to go. Make another for the customer. I need to go now. I'll put the cost of the pie against your bill from me--I'll be working for you until this is done."

Stone's mind was moving at light speed. He had to get a plan together. He thought he needed his gun: but then again why? Bullets cannot hurt him. More than likely the only bullet that would kill him might come from his own gun, fired by his own hand. He walked outside and mounted his bike, then he phased walked to the inside of his garage.

He got off the bike and called Buck, "Sorry buddy, change of plans, can you meet me at my home office?"

"Why not, who needs to eat anyway."

"I'll have a pizza waiting," Stone finished.

Evil will always seek to wear a disguise. The Mafia took on the mannerisms of the Beati Paoli to hide their treachery, just as corrupt governments wrap their duplicity in a flag and call it God's will.

11

FROM ANGELS TO BASTARDS

Back at Stone's house, Buck walked into the kitchen. There was an opened box with a pizza inside and an opened bottle of Miller waiting for him.

"Sorry about the change of plans. Look Buck, this is what I know; Alfredo's father is a police officer in Palermo. A few weeks back, he left his office to arrest a mafia Don and his capos for murdering a judge that would not take a bribe. As a result, those same people kidnapped him and now they are demanding the kind of money Alfredo does not have. Otherwise they will kill his father."

"What you mean to say is, no matter what, Alfredo's father is dead."

"Yea, that is what I mean, unless we can use this new ability to develop a plan to get him out."

"I'll beat a million dollars you have a few ideas already."

"Some, but I have to learn more about their organization and their motivations—besides just greed and ego. I simply cannot jump in and grab him. First, I have to know where he is, before I can phase walk to him. Moreover, just releasing the father from his jailers will only delay the inevitable; we need to destroy their entire infrastructure in such a way it can never rebuild; or worse yet, retaliate. These buffoonish oafs are superstitious with fusty religious facades; maybe we can develop a plan that takes advantage of those weaknesses. Perhaps we can even convert them into true believers."

"Stone, our Seal Team worked a lot with the ATF, the DEA, and the FBI. They all had bull's-eyes pasted on the backs of the international mafia organizations. I had to learn a lot about those scumbags and how they operate...as well as the mafia operations.

"The term mafiusu use to mean something beautiful or special in the Italian language. A man's tie or his large round belly was mafiusu; even a beautiful woman's eyes; or an especially beautiful day was referred to as mafiusu. That is until 1860, when an Italian playwright used the word Mafia in the title of a play describing crime organizations in the jail system. By 1865 the government that was trying to crack down on crime, started to use the term Mafia and mafioso to describe the gangs. Now the use of the word mafiusu to describe anything beautiful just is not done.

"The mafia, or to use the sexier term Cosa Nostra, has a simple organizational plan. They have defined territories with a boss or a Don who is elected by their group or clan. If the Don dies or is arrested, an underboss takes over. A Consigliere watches over the finances for the group and is a highly respected and experienced impartial advisor to the Don.

"Each subdivision in the territory has a Capo (Captain) sometimes called a capodecina or caporegime. Under the Capos are soldiers that do the dirty work like murder, extortion, muggings, bribery. Then finally, there are associates who are merely tools that help to expand the mafia's influence. These are the crooked cops, the corrupt politicians, low life thieves, or a degenerate businessman, with bad habits, illegal vices, and a lot to lose. Everybody pays a portion of their proceeds up to the next level. It is a lot like the Amway model, but with more guns and broken legs added.

"The low level associates and the soldiers know each other. In most cases, depending on the Clan's size, the lower levels never know anyone higher than the person that supervises them. That is unless stupidity and egos take over. Then you end up with Teflon Dons or other types of media hounds.

"Sixty years ago, commissions were formed whose purpose was to stop turf wars that disrupt business. The commission is comprised of the Dons that represent specific territories.

"I think most of the Mafioso today has learned their lesson and went back underground. They are even telling the press the mafia does not exist anymore. The Justice Department helps them out by televising to the public; their tax dollars broke the mafia's back. This obvious lie only helps to give the mafia the time it needs to heal and rebuild.

"The switch from the campaign of violence to a campaign of quietness is called *pax mafiosi*. The gangster Bernardo Provenzano started this practice just before his capture and arrest in 1995. Provenzano, acting as the head of the Commission, halted the campaign of violence and the internal wars that were so prevalent before that time.

"The origins of the Mafioso began in Sicily when rich absentee landowners needed someone to take care of their properties. They hired influential community leaders called Gabelloti to protect the land and its assets. The Gabelloti would hire Campieri to do enforcement and collect taxes from those using the owner's property. This protection cost the owners of the land a percentage of the taxes.

From this, everything expanded into what we face today. After a while, these organized groups started to control gambling and vices; extortion money soon evolved. The code word for this extortion money became pizzo. The term derived from the Sicilian word pizzu, meaning beak: to wet someone's beak, "fari vagnari 'u pizzu," is to pay protection money. Then after a while, drugs slid into the mix of lucrative revenue generators.

"There are many small organized criminal groups in southern Italy all lumped under the moniker mafia: the most notorious is of course the Cosa Nostra: meaning 'Our Thing' or 'This Thing of Ours.' There is also the 'Ndrangheta in Calabria, and the Camorra in Campania.

"There are legends of vigilantes with roots going back to 1698, during a time when control of Sicily passed first from being under Spanish rule, then to Piedmontese, then Austrian.

"In the beginning, local groups were formed to deliver justice for the people because the throne, or the seat of government, was always so far away and not able to do much for the villagers. That was when the State sanctioned the 'Arm of the Justice' or the 'Braccio della Giustizia.' This may have also been the first origins of I Beati Paoli (The Blessed People of St. Paola): small groups of hooded clandestine clansmen who carried out vendettas on behalf of perceived crimes committed against both individuals and the community. They fought against corrupt government, thieves, and the church during the inquisition. As the legend goes, even the peaceful monks became members because the corruption of the church was so bad.

"Because of all the injustice and the corruption in the Italian and the Sicilian governments aggravated by the lack of honorable soldiers or policemen, the male villagers formed this clandestine group that would avenge any kind of injustice and help to get back land, honor, or property stolen from the other villagers and their families. These were truly wise, brave, and incorruptible men—angels of honor.

"The irony here is that the work of true men of honor, who sacrificed their lives and livelihoods to protect others and their community, has been tarnished and confused with selfish slim who delude themselves that the crimes they now commit earns them honor and respect. Television series and movies exasperate those delusions seemingly glorifying the crimes, while dismissing the painful injury, and lack of justice their victims endure.

"If the Beati Paoli were caught, during the inquisition, they would be summarily killed without any type of trial. The deaths were very public and without mercy, meant to deter others from joining the group.

"All the members were bound by Omerta': a code of silence and secrecy that forbids the Beati Paoli from betraying their comrades to the authorities. The penalty for this transgression was death, and relatives of a pentiti (a turncoat) could be murdered. A few hundred years later, the Mafia with roots stemming from the gabelloti and campieri, also adopted this code of silence.

"Members were not allowed to associate with police or judges. They could not be related in any way to them either. The exception was when members corrupted the individual officers as necessary to gain much needed information or gain some other edge against a government or church. Those corrupted officials became tools easily blackmailed if they refused to do a favor.

"In the very beginning of the Beati Paoli formation, it took two like minded people to form a clan or group. Within the entire clan, only two people knew each other--the recruiter and the recruited. Everyone wore hoods during introductions or meetings: their identities constantly hidden. Only one person in a clan would know another from a clan in other villages. If anyone was arrested, this rule ensured only two people in a clan could be identified.

"Today's mafia follows a similar rule when it comes to introducing one inducted person to another. Even if an inducted mafia member knows another by reputation, he cannot introduce or expose himself as a member. He must go through another person that confirms and also witnessed that a member has truly gone through the initiation."

"Thanks. If I can sum up what you said Buck, what we have, in short, is a group of pious, overly delusional, superstitious, street-smart, business savvy, egotistical, arrogant crooks that would steal from homeless cripple veterans or old ladies if it puts a penny in their pockets.

"You may not think so Buck, but that really helped me to picture a long range plan that could shut those bastards down for a long time."

"What are you thinking?"

"Las mano del Diavolo."

All Buck could think to say was, "Oh my! Could I have another Miller with this pizza, please?"

When two hearts beat in harmony, notes can never be played in secret, and the occasional note played off key is soon forgotten.

12

THE DEVILS HAND

"So what's up partner, what's our next move?"

"Still working it out Buck, the first thing we need to determine is where Alfredo's father is being held hostage. We also need to understand more about my abilities and if they will last. I would hate to be jumping from one place to another and have it stop working. I like my existing atomic arrangement and I am not sure I would enjoy an eternal limbo   either."

Buck laughed, "Having second thoughts about your superpowers? Stone what happened at Doc Rick's office?"

"The MRI showed that my entire left brain is aglow. Like a big flashlight in my head."

"Always said, you were bright."

"He also helped me to understand a little bit more about the physics of what is going on. Every time I phase walk you get older, I do not age as fast."

"Hey, that isn't fair."

"There are probably a lot more things I can do. Last night I took a tumor out of Janet's breast: I can actually look inside of a person's body and see cancer. Buck it is amazing."

"I guess so. What did Janet have to say about the surgery?"

"I didn't tell her about it. She was asleep."

"That's rude."

"I am not ready for her to know yet. There are things that could still go wrong. Nonetheless, back to Alfredo, we need pictures and lots of them. I can only go places that I have seen."

Stone picked up his phone and called Alfredo, "Alfredo do you have very recent pictures of your father's home and what he looks like. Plus, any pictures of where he works for instance?"

"Yes, Sassolino, they are at my house. Linda is there now. She can bring them here soon."

"No, tell her to stay there. I am a few minutes away. Call her and tell her I will be stopping by to pick up the pictures."

"Ok, Sassolino."

Stone hung up and turned to Buck.

"Buck I am going to get the pictures. See if you can learn more about Palermo and the surrounding areas: most importantly the organization there. Perhaps your buddies can share some intelligence on the crime organizations they know about."

Stone jumped to the front door of   Alfredo and Linda's house—it took just a blink of an eye to get there. Stone reached out and rang the doorbell. Inside the house, the phone was also ringing.

Linda answered the door with the phone next to her ear. "Sassolino, boy you fast. Alfredo just said you coming by. I hope you go slower with the girls, Sassolino." Linda turned and began to walk back toward the living room but kept looking at him from the corner of her eye with one eyebrow cocked   upward.

She began to speak into the phone. "Ok, Sassolino is here. I get him the pictures, bye-bye." Turning back to Stone, Linda said, "Come in, can I get you something to drink?"

"No thank you, I am in a hurry. I really need as many pictures of Alfredo's father, his house, and the areas around Palermo where he works."

"Ok, you take these and go then. You be careful with those."

It was obvious to Stone that Alfredo had not told Linda of his father's kidnapping. There must have been a reason. Linda and Alfredo worked as thought they were a heart with a single beat. There were never any secrets.

Stone picked up three big albums of pictures. He opened the top one and the first image he saw was a police officer decorated with all his metals.

"I assume this is Alfredo's father?"

"Si that is Roberto. A strong man; yes?"

"Si, he certainly looks strong and proud. I have to go, thank you."

Stone walked outside as Linda closed the door behind him. He walked down the road out of site of her house and then phased walked back to his apartment. He ended up in the kitchen, just as Buck had his head in the open refrigerator looking for something to eat.

"Yo, Buck!"

Buck jumped up and hit the back of his head on the freezer.

"Damn Stone, you need some kind of warning bell around your neck. Darn, that hurt!"

Stone blew it off and walked back into his office with the photo albums. They both started looking thru them.

Buck went to Google Earth on the computer and zoomed into Palermo. He entered the address that Alfredo gave them for his father's home. Stone found some pictures of the interior. Stone turned and looked at Buck.

"Ok, I am going to Palermo to acquaint myself with the locals. See you in a bit. Can you work on the organization?"

"Don't worry about me, I'll do fine. Be safe."

Stone once again looked at the building that contained the apartment of Alfredo's father and concentrated on the interior of his living room. Instantaneously, he was in the Sicilian apartment 5328 miles away: maybe not at the speed of light, but still fast enough to beat a speeding bullet.

After walking around the apartment for a few minutes, looking for clues, he walked out the door and started down the stairs to go outside. An older woman stopped him on his way out, trying to talk with him in Italian.

Stone reached into his pocket pulling out his Android phone and opened the 'Talk to me Cloud' application. He selected the English to Italian translation and then was ready for a conversation. He spoke into the phone while looking at the inquisitive face in front of him.

"Excuse me Signora; I am a very good friend of Roberto's son. Can you help me find Roberto?"

After asking that, he turned the phone towards the woman allowing her to read his question in Italian and hear the phones digital voice repeat, in Italian, what he said.

"Mi scusi signora Sono un ottimo amico del figlio Roberto. Cerco Roberto mi puoi aiutare?"

Her eyes widen as if magic were happening right in front of her. "Cosa penseranno di prossima?" What will they think of next?

Stone continued to ask her questions and she would gingerly speak her replies into the phone. The conversation lasted about four minutes before Stone had some of the information he needed.

She had last seen him enter a van with two men from another village. She had never seen them before. He did not look concerned when he was with them.

Stone told her Mafioso kidnapped Roberto and if not found soon, he would die. She asked him in Italian, "What can be done?" Stone suggested that she spread the word that an American is here to kill the cowards that sleep with goats and offended his friend Roberto. Spread the word that the American is wearing a red plaid shirt with blue jeans and hiking boots. He told her to spread the rumor only, do not get otherwise involved. He wants the Mafioso to become very mad at him and to come looking for him. He will be easy to find.

Stone said his goodbyes to the gentle lady and began to walk to the police station. There he met with il capo della polizia-- the police chief.

Stone held his phone up for the Captain to hear. "il capitano si parla inglese?" (Captain do you speak English?)

"What can I do for you?" Toys did not impress the Captain of the Police.

"Captain, my name is Stone Richards; I am a friend of Officer Roberto's son, who now lives in America. Do you know Roberto has been kidnapped?"

Stone was watching very closely for the Captain's expression to change: he was looking for any signs of lying: a twitch, a glance down and to the left, touching his face, curling or biting his lips, folding his arms anything that indicated his possible involvement.

The Captain looked behind Stone for any other person that might be listening. "Come with me outside."

The Captain and Stone went outside and started to walk down a narrow cobble stone road towards an outside café.

"Mr. Richards please tell me what you think you know."

"I know for sure I have a friend in America that is very worried; and that someone called him saying his father has been held for ransom; and if money is not delivered his father would be killed. We are still waiting for the next call and proof of life."

"That is not how it works here. His father may already be dead. But yes, Roberto has been missing."

"Do you have any idea who took him?"

"Yes I have a few ideas, but not enough information for warrants to search private buildings and farms."

"Are the judges dirty here?"

"Yes some."

"Do you know, with certainty, which judges are not corrupt?"

"I think so, Si."

"Can you show me the likely places where Roberto may have been taken and can you also show me pictures of the members of the local Cosa Nostra clans?"

"Yes I can, but not in the office. Some of my officers are corrupt but I also do not have enough information to fire or arrest them. They are very careful not to provide the evidence I need. Showing pictures of Mafioso to a stranger may alert the corrupted officers to my suspicions. Then Roberto will surely die, so they can remove any evidence of their involvement."

"Captain I have some powerful friends who work in the shadows. They call themselves '**Las mano del Diavolo.**'

"**The devils hand?** I have never heard of these people before."

"Neither have I until just this morning. I have never met them; they work out of sight like the Beati Paoli. I am also told if you ever did meet one of them it would be your last breath; especially if you were not initially invited by an ordained member."

"Just like the mafia Mr. Richards. So what is the difference?"

"They are lead by a man the others claim is the devil himself. He can appear and disappear at will and can reach inside of your chest, remove your heart, and show it to you moments before you die. They formed to bring back the honor the Cosa Nostra has stolen from the legend of I Beati Paoli. Once again the Villagers will have their Robin Hood to admire and lean on."

"Mr. Stone I am not prone to believe in fairy tales."

"I would never ask you to believe in tales. Just believe when the changes begin, you will have a friend in **Las mano del Diavolo.**

"Captain, if criminals were delivered to your jail would they get a fair hearing; or will the judges let them go?"

"That would be up to the judge that is selected for the trial. It is impossible to say. It also depends on the evidence."

"It would seem to me, Captain, the criminals would have to confess their crimes before any trial, and then plead guilty at the hearing."

"Si, then for sure they would serve a sentence. But then they would also be considered mad."

"Perhaps, Captain, but then again they might be seen as truly repentant.

"When can I see the pictures of the Mafioso you suspect of kidnapping Roberto and get their addresses? Also, can I get any current aerials you may have of their homes or ranches?"

"See this café? Meet me here in two hours."

Stone and the Captain did not shake hands, they nodded at each other as the Captain sat down and ordered a coffee as Stone continued to walk-away down the ancient hand built roadway.

When Stone turned the corner into a dead end alley he looked around to see if anyone was watching. There was no one. Stone phase shifted into a moment that from an outside perspective, seemed to freeze the time he occupied. His two-hour wait would seem to him as though only a second passed.

Without a goal, common to all in a community, a nation, or all of humanity there will always be inequality. Someone will always be losing or always be gaining. With a common goal, no one is losing or winning because every person's eye is focused on the goal, not self-interest.

13

WHEN SMART MEN DESTROY WORLDS

Alfredo's grandfather was a master cobbler. He worked day and night fixing shoes or making brand new ones for this friends and neighbors. He used the finest leathers gathered from around Sicily for his shoes and boots. The heels were made of wood that made distinctive sounds on the cobble stone streets of Palermo. The sounds were unique to the size of the shoes and weights of the people that wore them: the attitudes they held about themselves and their worth amplified by the sounds coming from their shoes pounding against the stones.

Alfredo's grandfather prided himself in knowing the sounds made by many of his friends as their heels made contact with the rock. From his shop, he would call out greetings to them, as they walked by his shop door.

"How you-a-know it was me, you-a-magician or a cobbler?"

"It's the attitude of your walk my friend." He would say.

A payment for work in this poor village was with fowl, a goat, vegetables, milk, butter, and mostly with a bottle of fine wine.

There was always plenty of wine stored in wooded casks at the poorest of homes. On a few occasions, his richer patrons would pay him with coin. Those were always horded away. In this village, the main currency among the poor was food or services.

Alfredo's father worked as a cobbler's apprentice for many years and learned the trade from his father. He also worked as a tailor's apprentice with a man next door. Alfredo's father was enterprising and knew people needed suits and shirts to match their fine shoes made in his father's shop. One day Roberto would own a store with apprentices working for him and the store would sell fine clothing and handmade shoes.

In these early years, the government was never able to provide protection against thieves or vandalism. There were not enough taxes to pay the police properly. So many times, it was the government officials or the police themselves that were the thieves or vandals. It was how they made their living and were paid for their services. The Beati Paoli that once stopped that kind of corruption and injustice is now a thing of the past.

In these modern times, the bastards in the mafia now took over the role once played by angels. The Dons allowed just enough money to trickle down to the poor, and the church, so that there would always be a few people talking about their good deeds. They had infiltrated the police departments, the judicial systems, and the politics. The Dons were now the large landowners that collected the taxes through the thugs they hired to intimidate the villagers into paying the pizzo through fear and violence.

Many times because of his excellent work, the Dons personally protected Roberto's father. The Cobbler always did his best work for the Dons and charged them very little. Until one day, a new rival gang entered Palermo and started to threaten the business owners.

The new gang insisted on protection money for their services. Alfredo's Grandfather resisted and called upon his Don, his

Godfather, for help. It came too late. The shoe shop was burnt to the ground, as were other businesses that refused to pay.

The Don was eventually assassinated, and then his capos either switched to the new gang of thieves or were killed. The violence in the town grew with each new day resulting from vendettas and more resistance.

Mussolini added to the misery with his agrarian policy called "The Battle for Grain." It forced all Italian and Sicilian farmers to plant wheat in all their fields so Italy could stop importing it from foreign nations like the United States. Then instead of letting the farmers sell the harvest on the free market, government officials would come and take away what the farmers could not hide in the fields.

Worse yet, was the drain on the soils that growing wheat posed. Wheat sucked up the scarce minerals and nutrients leaving the farm soil barren, unable to grow even weeds for the cows.

Soon after the arson of the shoe shop and the depletion of the soils on the families' small farm, Alfredo's grandfather died of a heart attack: his death left the family without an income or a way to grow food.

Roberto had to find work where he could, but most shops would not hire him because of the bad blood his father left behind with the new mafia clan. Alfredo's father would remember this for a very long time.

Soon after the mafia violence began, Mussolini appointed Cesare Mori as the new Prefect to the City of Palermo. Mori immediately rounded up the criminals. He would even hold their families' hostage until the crooks gave themselves up. Thousands of Mafioso were jailed or killed. There was no mercy.

Cesare Mori had been so effective that he inadvertently began to uncover collusion between the Fascist regimes ran by Mussolini and the mafia in Sicily. The Dons in fact had been paying Mussolini to protect their land rights. For his hard work, Mussolini re-called Mori back to Rome. Mori was given a high seat on the senate. Before the scandal could be publically unveiled, Mori was rewarded very well for the risks he took.

As World War II began to escalate, Mussolini's army con-scripted Roberto. It was there he learned hand-to-hand combat how to shoot a weapon, and how to kill. Roberto took all the les-sons to heart and learned every detail. He became a good soldier who found his niche in life.

He viewed his role as a soldier, to be a protector of the peo-ple and his nation: there was nothing more, there was nothing less.

Near the end of the war, Roberto took a bullet in the leg. He went to a military hospital in Sicily. While there, the Allies con-verged on Sicily and eventually took over the island.

Thinking all the men in the prisons were political detainees the Allies let the prisoners out of jail. The Allies appointed some to be police officers, some judges, some mayors, and others govern-ment officials. They were in fact; Mafioso that Cesare Mori had pre-viously jailed for crimes against the villagers and Italy. There were thousands of prisoners. When the release was complete, the Mafia presence in the Sicilian government was stronger than ever.

Roberto eventually recovered and upon his return to civilian life joined the police force. He rose quickly in the ranks but pre-ferred to be in the field: always in the face of the mafia.

His most famous arrest after the war was Calogero Don Calo Vizzini: The man whose soldiers burned his father's shop down. That, however, was not the charge. Vizzini was charged with mur-dering police officers and a local judge. The evidence was over-whelming. After spending two years in jail waiting for a verdict, he was released. Free to go about his vicious crimes. Vizzini had pow-erful and forgiving friends in high government office in Sicily and Italy, but also America. He was instrumental in helping General Patton move swiftly through the villages and the complex mountain roadways: all suspiciously free of snipers and those that once supported the fascist Mussolini.

Vizzini used violence to steal from the rich like the Beati Paoli of old, and then share the wealth with the poor: but only after taking his very substantial cut from the spoils. This was how he justified his benevolence and calling himself honorable: this was how he justified murder.

Vizzini was the archetype of the paternalistic "man of honour" of a bygone age; that of a rural and semi-feudal Sicily that existed until the 1960s, when a Mafioso was seen by some, as a social intermediary and a man standing for order and peace.

Vizzini once explained how he viewed the mafia during an interview with the famous journalist, Indro Montanelli, in the Corriere della Sera in October of 1949: "The fact is that in every society there has to be a category of people who straighten things out when situations get complicated. Usually they are functionaries of the state. Where the state is not present, or where it does not have sufficient force, this is done by private individuals." Vizzini's known criminal activities included 39 murders, six attempted murders, 13 acts of private violence, 36 robberies, 37 thefts, and 63 extortions. Nonetheless, he was a man of honor.

Vizzini died before sentencing: but his children and his capos continued to rule his massive domain.

Many years later, the government got serious about eliminating the mafia; once and for all. They built a giant secure complex and held the Maxi trials. Out of 474 Mafiosi put on trial, only 342 convictions stuck. In violent retaliation, the Mafia murdered a Palermo judge and his son, a prosecutor, and an anti-mafia businessman. The political allies of the Mafia were also murdered for failing to reverse the convictions as promised. Giovanni Falcone and Paolo Borsellino were two magistrates who spearheaded the crusade. Car bombs were used to publically execute them because of their efforts to destroy the mafia. It was because of these explosions that the villagers lost whatever remaining respect they had for the criminals and turned against the Mafia forevermore. Omerta was no more. Informants began to help the police find and capture the crooks. The Mafioso retaliated by kidnapping and killing more police and judges. This struggle has lasted for over 20 years.

That is the story behind the events that lead up to Roberto's kidnapping. He had found evidence and witnesses that tied a Don to the murder of another Judge. The Don's capos found Roberto and took him out of action.

On one hand, it was hard to disagree with Vizzini: sometimes it takes a small group of people to "Set Things Straight" when things get out of balance and government is powerless to change the status quo. Then, who could justify, except for a delusional mine like Vizzini's, the duplicity of enriching one's self while playing the part of Robin Hood: the deceit and arrogance behind that was just too obvious. Steal a lot from the rich and give pennies to the poor. In many cases, the government was in collaboration with the crooks. For Stone it was about breaking up monopolies and resetting the game board: things had to be set straight and the government was inadequate.

Examples of doing this abound in nature, especially in old growth forests where long lived trees shade out the bottom growth, never letting the younger new trees reach the sunlight they need to flourish. Young trees are kept in a strangle hold: their fresh new innovative ideas that might help to resolve difficult challenges that face a modern world; are kept from the light of day.

When old growth trees are cut down, the young saplings at the forests floor can now receive the suns light and are able to compete to be the first to reach the full sunlight as others watch innovative new ideas branch out and prosper.

Sometimes nature does the difficult work of culling the forest by using lightening, fire, disease, or other disasters. Sometimes a chainsaw does the work. But preferably, and not often enough mind-you, the old wiser trees that have survived by adapting to environmental change, begin to shed some leaves and branches and help to make room for the next generation. Using this strategy, the old trees may even live longer; for when their trunks begin to weaken they have a younger stronger neighbor to lean against that can help to carry the load proffered by other forces of nature. Regardless, it was time to cull the old growth and to make room for the new.

Stone's plan was beginning to take form: the Devil's Hand would slowly replace the power and influence of the Mafia's far reaching shadow.

It is difficult to consider something superstitious, when it is slapping your face with an opened hand, and the pain is real.

14

THE MOUSE TRAP

To Stone it seemed that only a second had past, but indeed, over an hour had gone by since he phase shifted to slow his reality. After he re-synchronized back with "real" time, he walked back out of the dead end alley and headed towards the café where he agreed to meet the Captain of Police.

He stopped in a small shop that sold bed linen and purchased a black silk queen-size bed-sheet and a black pillowcase. Then again, he set off for the meeting place.

Stone wore his red plaid shirt, his blue jeans, and his hiking boots. He had hoped the gentle old woman was doing her part and spreading the word that this crazy American wanted to kill the Mafioso that sleep with goats and kidnapped his friend.

"Mi scusi signore non vogliamo guai."

Stone held his Google phone up for the waiter to repeat what he just said.

"Excuse me sir, we do not want trouble here."

Stone spoke into the phone in reply and what he said in English translated into Italian.

"I promise, I did not come here for trouble, can I have an espresso and a Sambuca with a stuffed tomato and bread, please?"

The exchange continued as the phone interpreted.

"But Sir, there are people saying you are here to kill the Mafioso and that they sleep with goats. Those are very terrible things to say. They will not tolerate that."

"What I meant to say is that the mafia sleeps with male goats and steals from babies and old ladies. They are not men enough to satisfy a female goat."

"Oh Sir you cannot say these things they will kill you for sure."

"What I am worried about is that you will refuse to take my order for food and I will die of starvation. Will you fill my request please?"

"Si, but you have been warned."

"Thank you."

That settled the question for Stone. The gentle old woman was very effectively spreading the rumor. It would not be long before a soldier or capo comes to Stone to make their displeasure known.

"Hello Mr. Richards."

It was the Captain and he had a large envelope with him.

"Here are the photos, I have written on the back who each person is and what their rank is within the organization. On the aerials, I have written down who owns the properties. I hope this will help you. On another note, people are saying that you are openly insulting the Mafioso and their virilita (manhood)."

"Captain I want them to come after me. That way I can find out faster, who is in charge. It is better for them to come to me."

"But when they come now, it will be with a knife or a gun. You will not be allowed to live. I had no idea I was dealing with such a fool."

Stone smiled, "I will be ok, thank you for your concern."

"Mr. Stone I have to go now. Be careful."

Stone opened the package but did not take the photos out. He instead looked through them one by one while they remained covered up.

The waiter returned with the espresso, the Sambuca and the stuff tomato with bread. He would enjoy this small feast while soaking up the sun in the open-air café.

The surrounding buildings, some were homes, some businesses, were built with brick and old stone held together with mortar. It was obvious stucco had been applied many times over: still, there were areas where the brick and stone were exposed. Old wooden doors created barriers between the cobbled stone streets and the buildings interiors. It was a picture out of a travel magazine.

"Godere la festa," (enjoy the feast) the waiter said before returning to the kitchen.

Stone drank down his espresso and sipped his Sambuca while he savored the tomato stuffed with lamb, rice, and herbs baked with olive oil drizzled over the top. The bread was dense, hot, and fresh. This picturesque moment Stone wanted to share with a friend or lover: he was thinking of Janet. Perhaps he would bring her back soon: after all, he had recently accumulated many unused cosmic frequent flyer miles.

The thick sturdy walls standing in front of him were laid in the Phoenician age around 734 BC. It all started as a market to encourage trade and commerce. Then war after war passed ownership from the Greeks, to the Muslims, and then the Romans, and finally to the Christians. Some of the walls damaged during World War II remain grumbled; a testament of righteousness triumphing over unmitigated evil.

It was an amazing place to think, Palermo had a rich history dating back to the Prehistoric Age. In 1953, the archaeologist Bovio Marconi, explored the Addaura grottoes and found wall paintings of people dancing, depicting propitiatory rites, some viewed them as shamans.

Shamanism is an anthropological term referring to the beliefs regarding communications with the spiritual world. Shamans are messengers between the human world and the spirit worlds. They treat illness by mending the soul; somehow, alleviating the traumas that affect the spirit restores balance and wholeness to the physical body. A shaman also enters supernatural realms or dimensions seeking out solutions to problems afflicting a community. Shamans call upon other worlds to help bring guidance to otherwise injudicious souls, or to ameliorate illnesses of a human soul caused by foreign elements. They operate primarily within the spiritual world, which in turn affects the human world. The restoration of balance results in the elimination of the ailment.

Thousands of years ago, Shamans, claimed to have the ability to travel between these different worlds so that others could be helped. Today science calls them nuts: today, Stone is not so confident of what he knows.

So here, where Shamans once danced and asked the spirits for guidance to heal their community, Stone will introduce the devil's hand that will rip the heartbeat of evil from the village.

Stone motioned to the waiter for the check. The Waiter walked over cautiously.

"Sir, your tab has been paid by those gentlemen over there by the black van. They ask me if you would talk with them after you finish your meal."

"Thank you. The meal was excellent. See I told you there would be no trouble."

"Sir, I think there will be trouble for you if you go to them."

"Thank you for your concern. Be well."

Stone stood up and walked towards the black van with two well-dressed men standing next to the opened side door. They spoke English.

"Did you enjoy your snack Mr. Richards?"

"Indeed, I did, thank you. Thank you for the meal, and may I ask who you are?"

"We are those you call capra amanti."

They opened their coats exposing holstered weapons. "We want to talk with you, would you step into the van?"

Stone knew this was not going to be a typical conversation, but then he intended to do all the talking anyway.

"Sure."

Stone got in the black van after which his abductors closed the door. The van began to drive down the narrow streets on its way out of town. As the van passed the last building and the road narrowed to a single lane with steep cliffs on either side, Stone reached over and touched the drivers arm; they both phase walked to a cliff just one hundred feet above the river of molten lava inside the giant lava dome on Stone's Pacific island.

The cliff shelf was only three feet wide and five feet long. The walls were smooth. Nobody could climb the walls. The "skylights" were just small dots on the ceiling perhaps a thousand feet or more higher.

Stone said and did nothing but leave the wide-eyed terrified driver on the cliff to think about his fate. Then he phase walked back to the moving van where the passenger was desperately trying to steer and simultaneously stop the van without wrecking. Stone waited patiently for the passenger to fulfill his immediate task.

When the van finally stopped, Stone picked up his package of photos and his package from the linen shop before grabbing the passengers arm. The passenger was wide-eyed and could not speak. His cool confident demeanor had vanished. Stone took the passenger to the same cavern with a view of hell's eternal fire, and left him on another shelf far out of sight from the other unfortunate participant in this plot.

Afterwards, Stone phase walked back to his house where Buck was waiting.

"Here you go Buck. All we should need to know."

As Buck started to thumb through the photos, Stone picked-up scissors from the desk; next he pulled the black sheets from the bag.

"Are you going to fill me in on what you are doing, ole buddy?" asked Buck.

"I am getting ready to start convincing Mafioso they need to repent before they fall into hell's fire."

"And how, pray tell, are you going to do that?"

"Right now I have two perspective converts literally stewing on shelves in that lava dome we visited on the island. From their perspective, I am sure it looks exactly like they imagine hell looks like. Once I get these sheets cut up, il Diavolo (the Devil) will pay a visit and offer them a few choices: fully repent and pay restitution to the poor; or spend an eternity in hell."

"What do I do with these pictures and maps?"

"Can you use some of your resources to find out which one of those characters might have kidnapped Roberto? The Captain of the Police in Palermo knows me; use my name if you need to talk with him. Right now, he thinks I am a nut. That should change in a few hours. So now, how do I look?"

"Like a nightmare that jumped out of an old Jim Crow story."

Stone had cut eyes holes in the black pillowcase and tied the corners into knots so they looked like horns. He put the pillowcase over his head to check the fit. He then cut a hole in the center of the bed sheet and slipped it over his head. The sheet dragged the floor and covered his shoes but his arms still looked too human.

To cover his arms he walked over to the closet and after removing the sheet and his shirt, he selected a black long-sleeve t-shirt and put it on. He then put on some cloth black gloves. After that, he again put on the pillowcase and the black sheet. He was done. In the darkness of the cave, all that the unrepentant criminals would see is death.

Buck made a query, "You are going to be in a cave, correct?"

"Yes."

"Then why not put a battery operated red light inside the hood. That would make your eyes look like they are glowing red."

"Fine idea thanks. You got what you need Buck?"

"Yea, I forgot to tell you, Janet has been trying to call you. She sounds pretty excited."

"I bet."

Stone phase walked to the driver first. He was standing up against the wall shaking and already deathly afraid. He screamed aloud when il Diavolo suddenly appeared with glowing red eyes. For effect, and to establish credibility il Diavolo reached into the driver's chest and squeezed his heart for three seconds causing the man to fall to his knees crying in pain. Il Diavolo still did not say a word. Then the driver began to weep as he spoke?

"What is this hell? Am I dead? What about my family?"

Still no sound from il Diavolo.

"What do you want from me? Why do you stand there?"

Il Diavolo decided now was the time to speak, "You have a choice, repent and pay restitution, or stay here until you fall into the eternal flame."

It was like purgatory. The cliff was a place where you could contemplate your sins and perhaps even get a chance to redeem yourself and enter heaven.

"What do I have to do?"

"Give me your gun hand."

The driver held up his right hand, il Diavolo grabbed a hold of it squeezing hard. Then il Diavolo reached into the drivers hand near the wrist and broke the hand bones loose from the arm. Finally, il Diavolo pulled all the bones from the drivers hand: leaving only formless flesh and muscle flapping from the end of the arm.

Il Diavolo showed the driver what use to be his hand bones and then threw them into the molten lava that was lurking below: the driver could only cry louder and shake harder with fright.

Il Diavolo spoke again, "You will never again hold a gun, you will never again steal, and you will never again harm another. This is the mark of the devils hand."

"Yes I promise," swore the driver as he continued to scream in pain.

"You will sell all your belongings and collect all your money and give them to the poor."

"Yes I will," again swore the driver.

"You will walk to the Captain of Police and confess all your sins completely."

"Yes I will, I swear," cried out the driver.

Stone immediately phased walked him to the cool pool of water with the waterfall still flowing and tossed the driver into the pool. The driver again screamed in shock and horror. However, as he looked around, it appeared he was in the Garden of Eden.

"What is this place, Heaven?"

"It is a place for you to drink, and remember. If you do not do as you swore, the fires of hell will consume your immoral soul. Now drink your fill and come to me."

The driver drank and then looked at the mass of formless flesh at the end of his arm. He cried, but knew it was better than the alternative.

Lurking above the driver in a coconut tree was old no claws, remembering when he too tried to take something from Stone.

Stone could not ask the driver where Roberto was because il Diavolo was suppose to know everything.

When the driver climbed out of the pool, Stone grabbed his arm and they phase walked to the front of the Palermo police station. Stone commanded the Mafioso to go inside, tell the Chief of Police about all his past sins, and repent. Then he can go about selling his assets from his jail cell and giving them all to the poor.

"What about my wife and children?"

"They cannot live from that which was stolen."

Then another unexpected thing happened. Stone did not want to go. He wanted to stay and listen to the confessions, but he wanted to be invisible; and that is what happened. It was involuntary. It looked to the driver as though Stone had just disappeared. Stone was beginning to understand all he had to do was think about what he wanted to do or needed, and somehow matter would shift to a phase that met his need.

As the driver slowly made his way into the police station, Stone phased walked to the passenger, presumably still in the lava dome. But he was not there. Stone looked around for any possible escape routes; there was only one. The passenger would never be heard from again.

Stone returned to the police station but remained invisible. He heard the driver reporting to the bewildered Captain.

"I have sinned, I have stolen from my neighbors, I have murdered my neighbors, I have bribed public officials and I want to make restitution and confess my sins, will you help me?"

"Who is your Don? Who are your capos?"

"I will confess everything, I swear. May I sit down and have some water?"

Salvatore Lucie was the drivers Don. Salvatore ordered numerous murders and had many judges and prosecutors in his back pocket. For years, Salvatore wetted his beak with the sweat of hard working community members. If they failed to pay the pizzo, they disappeared. Salvatore was a filthy parasite in the belly of Palermo. It was time for his extraction. Stone went back to his home to meet with Buck.

"Buck do we have photos of Salvatore Lucie?"

"Sure do, right here. How did it go with the costume?"

"Pretty well, if I say so myself; one buckled like a twig and sang like a bird. The other took a nose dive into the molten lava." I make a resplendent devil.

"I could have told you that a long time ago."

"Let's look on Google Earth to find where this pompous oaf lives so I can have a talk with him too."

Trickery and treachery are the practices of fools that have not the wits enough to be honest. Benjamin Franklin

15

DON GONE

Salvatore was an oafish fat slob. That was the most positive image Stone could paint of this crook after reading his file. He lived as he ate—as a glutton: swallowing completely, anything he could put his sticky fat fingers on. Stone was less than impressed with this Mafioso and was afraid that he would enjoy putting the pig down, just a little too much. He must remain under control and on point. There are only two goals, the first to get Alfredo's father back, and the second to rid this country of the Mafia. The only way that could happen is to scare hell into them. Il Diavoto was off to a good start.

Stone was outside the estate home of Salvatore Lucie. It was located in the center of a beautiful vineyard situated on five thousand acres of land stolen from French owners after the war. From this land, Salvatore and his capos rained terror down on the surrounding villages making the occupants pay for protection and do work for wages far below state minimums.

Il Diavoto was in his black bed sheets when he walked through the unopened front door and then walked from room to room looking for Salvatore. He had phased to become invisible.

He found Sal, like a squirrel readying for winter, stuffing his fat cheeks with pasta soaked in tomato paste and swilling some type of red wine. Over his vulgar protruding belly twice the size of a beach ball, he had a paper napkin dripping with red sauce and wine that spilled from his mouth. There was an effluvium all about him.

Sal was behind a desk in a large room lined with mahogany bookshelves filled with reference books, law books, and first addition novels. French doors lined an outer wall that looked out over a veranda and a thousand acres of rolling hills filled with grapevines. Il Diavolo began to speak; but could not be seen.

"Salvatore, why would a fat pig like you need a book? Are those one of the few things you can't stuff into your fat cheeks?"

"Who's that? Why do you speak to me like that? I will have you killed."

"I don't think so pig boy. It is time to face your destiny."

Stone, still invisible, walked over, reached inside the pig's fat chest, and began to squeeze his heart muscle.

Salvatore began to grab and scratch at his chest. His eyes began to bulge and he could not breathe. It was then that il Diavoto appeared.

"I do not mean to insult pigs, but you are truly a fat evil swine Sal, and now it is your turn to pay the pizzo for your sins."

"Halt," yelled a bodyguard.

Il Diavoto kept his grip on Sal's heart muscle while turning his head to look at the guard. There was a machine pistol pointed at him. All the guard could see were the Devil's red eyes, and the Devil's arm disappearing into his Don's chest.

Stone could hear himself think, "Point your gun at your kneecap. Pull the trigger." That is what the bodyguard did. In a dreamlike trance, the bodyguard blew his own kneecap off and then fell to the ground crying out in pain.

Il Diavoto turned to Sal and slapped him in the face. "Pay attention Salvatore. You ready for a trip to hell? I'll come back for your guard in a minute." With that last thought, both were in the lava dome on the ledge, overlooking the river of flowing hot crackling lava.

Salvatore was shaking and trying to throw-up. Il Diavoto's eyes were glowing redder in the cave's darkness, and Sal just knew he was in hell. His legs gave way and he passed out.

Stone leaned Sal's fat limp body against the dome wall and returned for the guard. Without speaking il Diavoto took the bodyguard to another ledge and then went back home to talk with Buck.

Stone was in the kitchen when he took his hood off. He opened the faucet and filled a glass with water. He took a drink.

"Buck, I am concerned I may be getting out of control."

Buck came into the kitchen.

"Stone, it is because you always question your own motives, is why you have become who you are. What do you think is wrong now?"

"I didn't want to play with that fat pig. I simply wanted to drop him in the pool of lava and move on. I was completely disgusted even having to look at him. I was losing my patience."

"Congratulations, you have once again, even with your superpowers, proven you are human. So what's new?"

"Salvatore and his bodyguard with only one kneecap are waiting it out in hell."

"What is this infernal obsession you have with removing kneecaps from bad guys? Wait a minute, you used a gun?"

"Not really, I just suggested the guard shoot himself in the knee and he did it. Kneecapping a bad guy forces him to remember why it happened every time they take a step. Maybe it will make them think twice before they hurt anyone else."

"WOW! That is scary, isn't it? You mean you can speak to a person's subconscious and make them do what you want?"

"I did it once. He had a gun pointed at me and I didn't want to find out if the bullet would pass thru me or not."

"Wait a minute; bullets can pass thru you also?"

"Apparently, it is a survival mechanism, my subconscious knows before I do there will be pain and shifts phases so anything solid will pass through me without harming solid tissue."

"You are superman!"

"Not really, I am a manifestation of what anyone could be if they have a higher level of concentration. There is nothing supernatural or mysterious about this. I am just surprised after trillions of years of evolution there is no recording of this ever happening before."

"I like superman, I can't even spell mannys-festation. That sounds nasty in any case."

"Any idea who has Roberto?"

"Nope, I did call el Capitan. He wants to talk with you. Seems some prediction you made came true. Crooks are walking into the jail house wanting to confess their sins and repent."

"It is the work of il Diavoto, and that is all."

"You're making a believer out of me."

"I'll be back soon; I have a meeting in hell."

Il Diavoto with his red eyes glowing appeared at the side of the sniveling Salvatore. Sal jumped to the side while making a sick gurgling sound and trying to curl up into a fetal position; but he could not for the presence of his fat beach ball sized belly.

"Sal you fat pig, do you know what purgatory is? Did you learn about that while you were stealing from god's church and the poor?"

Sal just wiggled his head in a way that looked something like an acknowledgement.

"This is a place where you have one last chance to rethink your sins and what you might have been able to do different in your sorry life. See those pockets; they do you no good here. See that river of fire down there?" Sal was too afraid to move and look. "Look at the destiny that awaits your sorry self, if you do not agree to change your life--Look now!"

With that said, il Diavoto grabbed Salvatore by his slippery neck and both of them went flying off the ledge towards the hot river of lava. Sal was screaming all the way down. Il Diavoto, just milliseconds before both plunged into the lava thought about the cool pool filled by the waterfall.

Sal was still screaming and kicking in the little pebbles that lined the shore of the pond when he realized he was no longer in hell. He turned around and faced Il Diavoto.

"Jump in the water Sal. Take a drink before you clean the shit out of your pants. This can be your Garden of Eden when you die Sal. On the other hand, you can burn for eternity in that river of lava: always thirsty, always hungry, always burning, but never dying. Go on take a drink; clean yourself up while I tell you how you can repent and save your filthy soul."

"What do I have to do, master?"

"Yea, right...first you must walk into the police station in Palermo and confess all the sins you have ever committed to the Captain. Then you must sell all your assets and give the proceeds to the poor. Will you do these things?"

"Yes I will, I swear."

"Come here Sal."

Sal tried to come out of the pond but his shaking was causing him to keep tripping and falling. He finally walked up to il diavoto.

"Give me your gun hand."

Salvatore gave the devil his right hand and both instantly ended up on the ledge overlooking the river of lava once more.

"I swear to you, I will do those things to repent."

"I know you will Sal, but there is one last thing: A reminder so you are never tempted to steal, kill, or hurt anyone again: a reminder to you and others that your past life was evil and self centered: a reminder to you that I will always be just a breath away."

With those words spoke, il Diavoto, tore out all the bones from Salvatore's gun hand leaving only rubbery flesh dangling at the end of his arm. He allowed Sal to look in horror at the bones, before they were tossed over the cliff, allowed to fall slowly into the molten lava. Sal could only shiver faster.

Then Stone thought of the front door of the Palermo police station. Stone was invisible, Salvatore was standing there alone, soaking wet, shaking in terror with his pants full of crap.

He slowly walked inside to confess his crimes.

He who fights with monsters might take care lest he thereby become a monster. And if you gaze for long into an abyss, the abyss gazes also into you. Friedrich Nietzsche

16

THE DARKNESS BEHIND THE LIGHT

Stone returned to his house.

"Buck can you call the Captain and ask him to meet me at the Café. He will be busy with a few prisoners, but ask him to cut it short. Tell him to ask where Roberto is being held. If they know, they will tell. Has Alfredo, called?"

"Not yet."

Stone picked up his cell phone and dialed the restaurant. After a few rings…"Hello Alfredo, have you received a call yet?"

"No Sassolino, I am concerned."

"My friend, things are going well. Keep hope. Let us know if you hear from those goat lovers."

"Ok, Sassolino."

"Buck, Sal was one slimy dirt bag nobody should ever have to touch. I need to go get the fleas off me. Is everything good here?"

"Yea, I'll let you know when I have something."

Stone stripped down and took a shower. He was still cringing from having to be anywhere near Salvatore. He was thinking he should have made him agree to lose 500 pounds as part of this penitence. Perhaps the prison food will do that.

The cell phone was ringing; it was Janet.

"Hello."

"Stone I have news, you won't believe it. The cancer is gone. They cannot find it anywhere."

"Honey, that is really good news."

"Do you think it was the herb paste you made?"

"Not really sweetheart, but nonetheless, we should make that a regular part of our diet and also cut down on meats."

"I am so excited, I want to celebrate."

"I do too, but Alfredo's father is in trouble and I am trying to help. I am hoping this will be over in the next few hours. I will let you know."

"Are you in danger?"

"The devil if I know. I will see you later on."

Buck called out, "Stone the Captain said he will meet you in the café in five minutes."

Stone changed back into his plaid shirt, blue jeans, and boots in order to trawl for more Mafioso and then left for the café.

The same waiter was serving that was there earlier. Stone walked up and sat at an outside table.

"Hello Sir, it is good to see you are ok. I thought your friends were not in such a good mood."

"Yea, I thought the same thing but I got them turned around. In fact, one walked over to the police station all by himself and confessed all his sins to the Captain."

"Really; why would he do that?"

"I was told because the devil literally took his hand away and then threatened to keep him in hell if he did not confess and re-pent, it was something like the Muslims do, but different. He called it the Devil's hand. Can you get me two espressos and two Sambu-ca."

"Yes, sir."

As the Captain came walking up the cobble stone roads, the waiter could be seen telling the kitchen staff what he just learned. The rumors will spread quickly.

"Mr. Richards."

"Captain; I already ordered for us if that is ok. Have you learned where Roberto is being held captive?"

"No, but it has been an interesting day, I have one capo and a very important Don that walked into my jail demanding they be arrested for their sins and they also want me to help them sell all their assets and give the money to the poor. How is that possible?"

"Roberto, Captain, did they tell you where he is?"

"They do not know. Is this the work of the Devils Hand? Each one had bones missing in one of their hands. There are no surgical scars. How can that be?"

"Captain, I told you this is a powerful group I work with. It is the Devil's hand. They are people you can trust. They have no other motive than to destroy corruption and help people find their common purpose for living. Do not be afraid of them."

"I am afraid of anyone who can turn those blood thirty thieves into babbling idiots. They are talking about being dragged into hell, and then afterward into the Garden of Eden: given a chance to save their souls. This is crazy talk."

"Will their confessions put them away in jail for the rest of their lives?"

"Most certainly they will."

"There will be more filling your cells later. First, we must locate Roberto. Time must be running out. No one has called his son, as of 15 minutes ago."

"Roberto was on the trail of the people who killed the judge. He kept his information to himself with my permission. We both knew that there are police in my unit that work with the mafia."

"Show me who they are. I will a talk with them."

The captain was well prepared; he had already become a believer in the Devil's hand. He gave Stone a list of names and photos of each officer along with their schedules and patrol routes. That was all il Diavolo would need.

"Captain, there is a black van on the edge of town. I am sure the prisoners will be glad to give the title to the police department. The keys are in the van."

After saying goodbye and paying the waiter, Stone went back to interrogate Sal's bodyguard. It was too late; the guard was lying on the ledge motionless. Stone reached down to feel for a pulse. There was none. It was likely he bled out from his leg wound. Stone stood there for a moment to think as he watched, mesmerized, by the river of boiling lava flowing by. It was making eerie cracking and popping sounds as the surface lava cooled, hardened, and then once again was broken apart and consumed once more. Stone remembered a quote by the writer Nietzsche, "...if you gaze for long into an abyss, the abyss gazes also into you."

Stone leaned over and pushed the dead body over the side. It banged on the jagged edges before plunging into the hellish river. There was no sadness or words about a life worth living: a life cut short. The body Stone discarded was a misguided waste of breath that stole the lives and dignity of many others. He had chosen his path; new verses from his life will not be missed. Stone returned home.

"Buck go home, it doesn't seem we can do anything more at this moment. I am going back to question some of the police that worked with Roberto. My guess is they know who did this."

"Stone I am here to the end. I don't need to go home."

"I know, but there really isn't anything you can do unless you can find a connection between one of these guys in the file and the murder of the judge. You can do that at your house."

"I feel helpless and I hate that, so I will just stay here and continue to run the backroom. Stone I have to be honest with you; I am feeling a little left out. I miss the action."

"I know you do Buck. Tell me what you want to do and I am in, right now however, I am popping from one place to the other so fast no one can keep up. What I really need to help Roberto, is information. We need to find out where he is or who has him: I don't care which one; either will get the job done.

"How is this, why don't I introduce you to the Captain in Palermo and you guys can work on finding the information we need?"

"Now that's what I am talking about. Let's go."

Both Buck and Stone phase walked to the front of the Palermo Police station. Buck had all the photos and maps the Captain had previously given Stone. As they entered and walked towards his office, the Captain eyed Buck warily.

"Hello, Mr. Richards, this is unexpected."

"Captain, excuse the intrusion, I know you are busy; can we talk privately in your office?"

"Please come in."

"Captain this is Buck."

"Buck who?"

"Just Buck Captain, everybody knows me just as Buck."

"Captain," Stone continued, "Buck is a retired navy seal commander, he comes to us with very high references within the American government. You are free to verify them. He can be fully trusted. We need help finding Roberto and Buck has the contacts and expertise to make that happen."

"What can he do to help? We are in Sicily not the United States."

"Il mil ufficio e' il mondo, el Capitan." Buck surprised even Stone with his response to the Captain.

"The fact that the world is your office and you speak perfect Italian still leaves the question; what can you do to help?"

"Captain you are the boss," replied Buck, "You point and I jump. I have researched the men in these photos and got what information the FBI and the CIA has on them. I have failed, however, to find connections to Roberto's kidnapping."

"Mr. Richards, what does your group think?"

"They are also at a loss. Nonetheless, they are working with the files you gave me concerning the suspected officers."

"So we are no further ahead than before," said the Captain.

Stone spoke up, "Not necessarily, we have two Mafioso screaming about a Devil who stole their hand and that must be scaring someone, and there are two other killers that have disappeared for good."

"Who are they," asked the Captain.

"They mattered before because they hurt people, but they don't matter now Captain. They are gone for good."

"Where?" asked the Captain.

Stone's only reply was, "Hell."

Stone continued, "Captain I need a cell phone with a local number so we can stay in touch. Next Buck needs a weapon. Today Americans are a target in Palermo until this is over. Remember, he is more highly trained than anyone on this island."

"Sure, sure, take this phone here. This is the number for my direct line: Buck do you know what this is?" The Captain reached into a desk drawer and pulled out a pistol.

"A stainless steel Beretta 92FS INOX: made for the Italian police and military and adopted by the US military in 1985. Cumbersome for people with little hands, but I don't have that problem."

"Yes, you are a specialist. Please be careful. I will also give you a temporary license in case someone questions your possession of it."

Stone broke in, "I have an idea, why don't both of you start splitting up the suspects in the police department and begin asking them questions about Roberto's kidnapping. Call me and let me know which ones need special attention. I can take it from there. However, and this is important, have them talk with the new prisoners first. Let them hear about il Diavolo and their experience."

Stone turned and walked outside. He was in his plaid shirt and jeans. He continued to trawl for Mafiosi, bold enough, or insulted enough, to approach him.

Buck had studied the files of the suspected police and had a general idea of what he was working with. Most of the police were family men barely making a wage to feed their children or to buy clothing. Most had small farms on the side to make extra income. Many were honest. The easy money spread around by the mafia, however, tempted some.

In the beginning, these prospects were only asked about schedules, or what investigations were going on behind the scenes. The small amounts of money they were given turned them into "tools" for the crime bosses. When the time came, they would become expendable; then they were required to commit murders, steal files, help to corrupt jurors, or stand by as homes or a business was broken into or burned.

The police chief called all the suspects into the hallway facing the cells that contained the Mafioso exposed to the Devil's hand.

"We have something mysterious happening in Palermo today. It is not explainable. As you patrol the streets this afternoon, I want you to keep your eyes out for anything that can help to explain what you are about to hear.

"These Mafioso have turned themselves in and they want to repent for their sins; someone or something has stolen the bones in their hand so they cannot sin again. This is Salvatore Lucie, you all know him as a wanted criminal that has murdered and stolen from many people."

"This is but one penalty for your sins," Salvatore held his arm up with the boneless hand flapping at the end. "The Devil himself took me to hell to show me what was in store for my damned soul if I did not repent. Then he showed me the path to salvation. I have seen the Garden of Eden it is beautiful compared to the fires and stench of hell. You must repent; we must all repent to save our souls."

The Mafioso driver walked to the front of his cell, "It is exactly as he said; the devil has black flowing robes and bright red eyes that are on fire all the time. He takes the bones in your hand to remind you he is only a breath away, if you fail to heed his warnings and sin again—THIS IS THE DEVILS HAND!" The driver also held his arm up showing everyone his boneless hand.

Buck shook his head and smiled, thinking to himself, "Damn Stone, what did you do to these poor bastards?"

Stone had taken ruthless killers and made them into babbling prophets screaming for everyone to repent and save themselves. The legend of the Devil's Hand will spread like fire in a pile of dry wood.

Out of the pool of seven suspected police officers, the Captain had his favorites for the crime and Buck saw body language that made him suspicious. Buck began to use his most formal Italian to speak.

"Captain I would like to question Luigi and Angelo, they were not able to stand still during the presentations by the Mafioso."

"Be my guest."

Buck turned to the small group and called out, "Luigi and Angelo, would you please talk with me for a few minutes?"

Both of the suspects turned to look at their superior officer.

"Please answer his questions; he is a friend of Roberto's."

"Hello guys; my name is Buck, do any of you have any idea what has happened with Roberto or who he was investigating for the judges murder?"

"Bingo," Buck thought to himself. Both officers, at the same time, looked down at the ground and tried to conceal their faces; one by scratching his nose, the other by scratching his ear.

"Come over here for a second, both of you."

Buck asked Salvatore and the driver to hold out their bone-less hands. Turning to the suspects, "I want each of you to hold one of those hands and then think for a minute before you try to speak again."

Neither Luigi, nor Angelo moved one inch.

Buck yielded so loud in Italian Salvatore fell backwards onto his cot and the Captain almost drew his weapon. "Come here and grab their hands you lying slim bags! I want you to know what is in store for you, if you continue to lie to me. The Devil himself will come drag you to hell! And I will piss on your grave if one hair on Roberto's head has been hurt!"

Angelo had a tear beginning to roll down his face. "Take Salvatore's boneless hand Angelo." Buck said more calmly.

Angelo took Salvatore's lump of skin and almost threw up. His entire body started to shake. "Tell him what he needs to know Angelo or your soul will burn in hell, I know this, I have seen it." Salvatore's words were the last straw for Angelo.

"Franco Rizzo, I borrowed money from one of his capos, I could not pay it back; they threatened to kill my family if I did not pay the money back or help them. All they asked was to know who was investigating the judge's murder. It seemed harmless."

Buck replied, "Well now one of your fellow officers may be dead. That doesn't seem harmless does it? Where is he?"

Angelo did not know. Buck turned to Luigi and yelled, "Where the hell is he you bastard?"

"I have no idea? Like Angelo I only know that Rizzo has him."

"Captain let's call Stone and let him know it is Franco Rizzo."

The Captain called Stone who was walking down the streets looking for trouble. After the call, Stone immediately went to his house and looked up where Rizzo lived, and then he once again put on his black sheets and became il Diavolo.

The Devil stopped first in the middle of the police station. He turned the heads of everyone in the room. Without a word, he walked over to the shaking Luigi and Angelo. Salvatore and the driver fell to their knees and started screaming, "It is him, it is him; it is the Devil, he has come to take us all to hell again."

The Devil held his hand out seemingly to stop the Captain from pulling his gun. Still without a word, the Devil touched Luigi and Angelo. Just as they disappeared in front of everyone's astonished eyes, they immediately reappeared on the shelf in the lava cave. The Devil left them both there, shaking, but not until he let them gaze into his shining red eyes. The Devil disappeared to find Franco Rizzo.

It was another large estate surrounded by mountains, lust green pastures, and vineyards. Unlike most estates in Sicily, Rizzo had spent a fortune on wells and irrigation. There were sheep scattered throughout the fields and Arabian horses. Rizzo had become well known for his purebreds. But not as well known as being a murdering Mafioso that only another thief could respect or do business with: there were enough of those that business remained good.

The Devil in his black sheets deliberately walked through the doors of the estate home and then became invisible. He walked over rustic looking quarry tiles and passed by ornately appointed walls with pillars that braced the tall ceiling. He was listening for any sound of movement or conversation. He found Rizzo in the Kitchen talking to someone on the phone, all Stone heard was...Kill him!

Il Divaolo, still invisible, put his hands into Rizzo's chest and began to squeeze off the lungs, not allowing him to take a breath. Rizzo tried to scream in pain but nothing came out. The devil held on. After 30 seconds of excruciating pain, the devil appeared in front of the blue faced wide-eyed Rizzo.

"Kill who, Franco? To whom were you talking with? Did you tell someone to kill the American, perhaps Roberto? Do you know you are a fool, and now your soul is damned?"

Rizzo could not speak he could only shake his head no.

"Then who; who is dying today besides you?"

Rizzo still could not speak. He could only continue to shake his head.

"Franco Rizzo it is time for you to pay for your sins, I am taking you to hell for your judgment you slimy piece of goat dung."

Franco and the Devil appeared on a wide shelf just 50 feet above the flowing river of lava. Angelo and Luigi could be heard screaming in fear maybe even pain; there was no way of knowing. The lava was still making the cracking and popping sounds. It was very close to what anyone would imagine hell to be.

"Everyone wants to repent when they see the eternal fires of hell, but then it's too late. What about you Franco you want to repent?" The Devil finally let Rizzo's lungs breath. He began to suck in air and gasp for more. Even in the dim pale light of the lava dome, Stone saw color come rushing back into Rizzo's face.

"Who are you going to kill Franco: Roberto; the Policeman who wants you in jail?"

"What's it to you?"

"You mock the devil you pig: are you really that big of a fool?"

Il Diavolo then reached his hand into Rizzo's chest once again but this time, to give him a different pain by squeezing his heart. "You like pain Franco: we can have an eternity of this if you would like."

Franco screamed and cringed from the pain.

"Try this flavor of pain, you are a brave guy, you must really like it, I call it the kidney crunch."

The Devil grabbed both of Franco's kidneys and squeezed. Franco's head flew backwards and he went down to his knees screaming in pain.

"Yes, yes! It is Roberto I have ordered him killed. What do you want from me?"

"Where is he?"

"He is in the basement of my horse barn."

"He better be alive, otherwise I will personally dip you inch by inch into the fires of hell that lies before you."

Stone phase walked to the front of the horse barn and ran into the building looking for doors that would lead into the basement. There was only one door. It led to something looking like a closet. He opened it and saw stairs leading downward. He jumped down the stairs two, three at a time. At the bottom there were four goons standing in front of one man tied to a wooden chair. The only light came from two light bulbs handing from thin electrical wires.

One of the goons had shot his weapon just as Stone reached the bottom of the stairs. Stone screamed as he realized what had just happen, "Noooooo...!"

Time instantly froze, but it was too late, the bullet was already existing Roberto's head. The skull was flying apart. Blood was everywhere. Stone walked towards the frozen gruesome picture.

Stone was trying to figure out what was happening. Time was frozen. There was no color; again, he could only see varying intensities of white energy; different shades of white with tints of blue or red were also present. In one direction he could see blue getting darker and in the other he could see reddish tints becoming a deeper red. As he walked towards the red, he could see the bullet and skull fragments fly further apart: if he backed up towards the blue, time seemed to reverse itself.

Stone immediately understood what he would have to do. It was the only chance to save Roberto. Stone walked towards the blue colors until he saw himself running back up the stairs. As he did so, the parts of Roberto's skull were coming back together and the bullet was returning to the gun barrel. Stone continued to move towards the blue hues until he was outside the barn. Then he re-started time.

Now Stone knew exactly Roberto's location. He phased jumped to Roberto, put his arm around him, and then phased walked him to the police station. When the gun fired, back at the barn, the bullet only found air. Stone was still il Diavolo to all who saw him in his black sheets. Everyone in the police station stood motionless as the Devil untied Roberto and set him free from the chair.

As Roberto cautiously stood up, the devil turned and pointed to Buck with his black gloved hand. When Buck walked up next to him, they both vanished to everyone's astonishment.

The Captain began to cross himself. Never having believed in such things before, the Captain was a convert now.

Positioned on top of a hillside overlooking the horse barn, where Roberto was once a hostage, Stone was still in his black sheets and Buck was shaking his head with a grin on his face. "Stone, you will never convince me you are not having a hell of a time: literally."

"It was amazing Buck, I actually reversed time, I saw Roberto's head blowing apart: without trying, I stopped time then reversed it. Can you imagine the possibilities?"

"Stone, can you imagine the lotto numbers?

"Forget that, I saw someone being killed and I was able to reverse that and change destiny. That is too much power for any one person."

"Let's discuss that later Stone, what are we doing here?"

"The four gunmen that tried to kill Roberto are in that building."

"Where is Franco?"

"He is cooking in hell at the moment, but I have not had a lot of luck with the shelf he is on. I have already lost two others today in that same area."

"That's too bad. What is next?"

"You wanted action; let's go have some fun with the bastards in the barn."

Stone and Buck phase walked to inside the barn. Stone found an empty feed sack and gave it to Buck, "Cut eye holes and put that on. Put another on as a shirt and hurry up."

Sounds of footsteps running up stairs were heard from behind the door. The gunmen were coming up. Stone grabbed Buck and both became invisible.

"Damn Stone that is too cool."

"Be quiet, Buck, they can hear us."

As Buck continued to fiddle with a disguise, all four gunmen entered the barn yelling at each other in Italian. Buck whispered the translation to Stone.

"They are accusing each other of letting the hostage go. One is saying no one let him go he just disappeared. Another is asking, who should tell Franco that Roberto just disappeared in thin air like a ghost. They are going to get in the SUV and drive to the house to tell Franco."

"Good hold on to me. I won't have time to take care of you also."

Stone and Buck walked over to the SUV and waited for the goons to get inside. When they did, Stone envisioned the SUV suspended over the end of the shelf where Franco should be standing. Stone touched the bumper. Everything and everyone touching Stone, including the contents of the SUV jumped to the shelf in the lava dome that was also holding Franco.

Franco was sitting down on the shelf blubbering to his self when they arrived. Then another strange ability was unveiled. Only the SUV was stuck in time, everyone around it, or in it, was in the same time-period. Stone now understood what he needed to do to achieve maximum results from his new abilities. It was all about concentration.

Il Diavolo let everyone inside the car get better acquainted with their impending doom. "Buck, let the gentlemen know they have reached their final destination and that they are on the edges of hell. They have five seconds to get out before I allow the truck to fall in to hells fire."

Buck complied and the very confused and afraid passengers were still reluctant to get out.

Stone generated a telepathic imagine in their minds, illustrating how the SUV was going to fall into the hot molten lava. After which they bailed out quickly and joined their former Don on the shelf.

When everyone was out, Stone let the SUV fall into the river of molten lava. It immediately caught on fire as it began to sink out of sight.

Luigi and Angelo could still be heard screaming out for help. The popping and cracking sounds seemed to be getting louder. The Devil's red glowing eyes began to peer at the four gunmen.

One gunman pulled his gun and shot the Devil in the chest. The bullet passed through harmlessly ricocheting off the rocks.

Buck said, "Well that question is answered."

The devil grabbed the gunman's hand and severed it from the arm. In front of everyone, he tossed the hand and the gun into the magma. The gunman began to scream and hold his handless arm.

The Devil transported him to his own shelf, as he also did for the other three. The entire cavern began to fill with screams and echoes for help. It would take some time for all the participants to become the Devil's converts. They would confess and repent, or they would die in the Devil's hell.

The devil returned to Buck and Franco. Franco was still blubbering in a fetal position. The devil reached down for Franco and told Buck to hold on. They all ended up at the pond. The devil pushed the fat Franco into the water. He went straight to the bottom and did not seem to want to move; perhaps he could not.

After ten long seconds, Buck was concerned and dove in after him. Buck pulled Franco out to where he was half in and half out of the water: Buck climbed out of the water and moved to the side. Stone looked at Buck simply saying, "Liberal. A real republican would have let the bastard drown or swim on his own."

The devil towered over Franco, "You have a choice you self-ish pig, you can go back to hell, burn forever and never die, or you can go back to Palermo, confess your sins, and repent."

"What must I do?" Franco said, while coughing out water.

"After you confess all your crimes, you must also give every-thing you have to the poor."

"I would rather die in hell."

The Devil did not even blink an eye; both he and Franco were back on the shelf. The Devil took both of Franco's hands and separated them from his arms. While Franco was looking at the Devil's red eyes, stunned and unable to speak, his severed hands were tossed down in front of him. Franco formed his mouth into a scream but did not make a sound.

"Here is your home for the rest of eternity Franco; when you are tired of this shelf, feel free to take a swim. While you are con-templating that, also think about this you greedy bastard; even if your pockets were full of gold, what good does it do you? You can-not buy me. If I wanted your gold, I do not need your permission. I would just take it: Just like you stole it from all the others."

"Wait, Wait!"

Stone ignore him. Instead, he left to collect the selfish police officers, "Are you ready to confess all your sins and repent?"

"Yes, we are, what do you want us to do."

"You will have to answer to Roberto and your Captain."

Stone took the couple to a jail cell next to the driver and Sal-vatore. No one saw the devil; they just heard the corrupt police of-ficers calling for help. Roberto and the Captain walked to them. Roberto walked forward, grabbed the cell door, and shook it to make sure that it was locked; then he turned and walked away.

Roberto asked the Captain, "What is happening here?"

The Captain replied, "All I know, it is called the hand of the Devil. Right now, I do not care, you are safe, and criminals are turning themselves in for prosecution. Why should we question that? Roberto, call your son, he is the one that brought this good fortune to us."

Roberto went into his office and picked up the phone. It rang a few times, "Hello, Alfredo's Paradiso."

"Hello Son, it is your father, I am ok. My Captain said you sent the people to rescue me. Thank you.

"Father, I am so glad to hear your voice, are you hurt?"

"Not at all son, we have a lot to talk about. Can I talk with you later? And thank you for sending your friends."

"What friends?"

Roberto had hung up before hearing Alfredo's question. When he turned around, il Diavoto was behind him.

"Do you want to meet with Franco Rizzo?"

"Who are you? You saved my life. Who..."

"Do you want to meet with Franco Rizzo?"

"Si, I do, where is he?"

Il Diavoto took him to the handless screaming Franco.

"He is yours, do what you want."

"Who are you?"

"That does not matter; you tell me what you want. Throw him into the fires of hell, or you can save him, his soul is yours."

"Save me Roberto, I will give you anything, anything."

"You have to give me your confessions."

"I will."

Then the devil spoke.

"And you will give all your wealth and property to the poor."

"I will. Roberto, save me please."

Il Diavoto leaned down and viciously grabbed Franco's arm while also touching Roberto. Franco began to scream and cry loudly. They all ended up in the police station, but the Devil was gone. Everyone in the police station stood watching the once powerful Don crying like a baby on the floor; his shaking body had lost control of its bowels. Both his hands removed.

The Devil returned to have a cheap beer with Buck. Buck was drying out next to the pond, and waiting for Stone to return. His nose helped to find the cooler full of Miller beer stashed behind some shrubs.

"Hello Buck."

"Wow, what a day, I have never seen something that amazing in my entire life Stone. Those poor bastards wouldn't steal a piece of candy if they were the only ones left in the store. This is a completely new journey for both of us. Thanks for inviting me."

"It was you that found out where Roberto was."

"Yes, but you had them pretty well softened up."

"Buck, I really am depending on you to help keep my head on straight. This thing worries me."

"Stone you don't give yourself enough credit. You could have easily left those crooks in the lava dome, but instead you con-

vinced them you were a devil and caused them to confess and repent. That was genius. For years, they will be convincing others
there really is a devil and a hell, and that everyone should stop doing wrong against others. Why in the world would you want to
listen to me?"

Stone took off his hood, "Because, Buck, sooner or later,
every saint has a devil that gets the better of them: with abilities
like these that must never happen. Moreover, continuing to pro-
mote a devil and hell only perpetuates humanities ignorance. That
only delays the day when the entire species will realize their highest
potential. Perhaps the prevalence of irrational superstition explains
why evolution has not bestowed this gift on the rest of humanity:
they simply are not yet responsible. That may be the reason the
right side of the brain filters out so much more of what the Universe
has to offer. It holds the species back until they grow up and decide
it is time to put away their security blankets. Every saint is influ-
enced by his or her own internal devil and the bias they grew up
amongst. Everyone must continuously get to know and question
their devil to stay ahead of its selfish desires. Speaking of selfish,
quit hogging the beer and give me one; or I'll send you to hell."

"Amen. Speaking of, did you get everyone out?"

"No, the gunmen are still in there. I am tired of dealing with
selfish idiots for the day. If I am lucky they will jump in the lava and
save everyone a bunch of trouble."

"Are you going to let them fry, or get them out?"

The answer was a foregone conclusion. It was not in Stone's
character to abandon anyone. No matter how worthless his or her
contributions to life may seem; everybody contributes. Every action
influences a life in a good way or a bad way; even the smallest of
actions contributes to the course of destiny. When any person says
a situation or another person is hopeless, they are simply slamming
the door in the face of God: the Librarian. Stone was convinced long
ago, if a God finally emerges from this primal soup of life, it would

be the sum total of all of humanities actions: the good, the bad, and the ugly. Stone will always contribute, with his last breath, to the better side of humanities nature. He was intent, not only to make a dent in the Universe; he intended to kick meaning into it.

"Damn, a devil's work is never done; let me finish my beer will you?"

After a few more beers and half a bottle of bourbon later, Stone became the devil once more, but this time with a slight smell of liquor coming from his breath; but then again he was the Devil.

While Buck took a swim and built a fire for a lobster dinner, the Devil went about getting the remaining Mafioso to agree to confess their sins and repent. In the morning, four more criminals with boneless hands were in the jail cells all asking to confess their crimes and to give their wealth to the poor.

While sitting around the fire with bellies full of lobster and Jim Beam the two friends gazed at the stars while puffing on a fresh Cohiba. Every stogie was smoked during the survey while Stone was gone; luckily, for them, the local Cohiba factory was right around the corner just 7000 miles away.

"What now Stone?"

"I think I have a handle on this sucker, so in the morning when I sober up a bit I will take the *Spiritus* to the Eau Gallie Yacht Basin and give it to Ed for repair."

"Why not now?"

"It would be irresponsible to phase walk while under the influence. What would that be anyway, PWWI, IWPW, WIWPW, UIWPW. Nonetheless, right now all I want to do is drink, smoke these cigars, and watch stars."

"You do remember the last time you did that? You were handed a hand full of ass!"

"Yes I remember; this time I am only watching slow moving stars."

For the rest of the night, the two friends enjoyed nothing more than each other's company and the senseless babble. It was a good time. They have earned the joy.

"Stone, I want to tell you one more thing before I pass out."

"And what is that?"

"I am going to ask Barbara to marry me."

"Good night, Gracie."

How simple and frugal a thing is happiness: a glass of wine, a roasted chestnut, a wretched little brazier, the sound of the sea.

Nikos Kazantzakis

17

BODHICITTA: MAY IT BE SO

In the early morning, before the sun even began to think about shining, Stone poured out of his hammock. He did not have the heart to wake-up Buck, although his boundless snoring had kept everyone else from sleeping.

After he stood up, the first thing he did was to bend over and pick up a few coconuts that had recently fallen. He tore off the husks and then broke apart a few nuts. He gave them to No Claws who was close by.

Stone noticed that his coconut crab friend was beginning to change colors. That meant he was close to shedding his exoskeleton and would once again have some front claws to peel and open his own coconuts. He wondered if the crab had learned to leave toes alone.

Like a stray dog, the crab adapted to and certainly learned to tolerate humans, more than likely due to the easy food. No matter the crab's reasons, Stone remembered the reluctant sacrifice the crab made so that Stone could live to fight another day. Opening nuts for the little monster was simply quid pro quo.

After watching No Claws scamper down the palm and begin to pick out the coconut meat, Stone phase walked over to Bagel Joes on Merritt Island. Joe was behind the counter. He was loading the metal shelve baskets with freshly cooked bagels. Stone ordered two opened faced lox sandwiches with onion, capers, and tomatoes on a toasted onion bagel with extra spicy mustard; plus two large coffees.

While waiting for his purchase, he pondered on the idea of how many carbon credits he could earn if he told people about his new abilities. Think of the gas that would be saved, the fossil fuels that would not clog the atmosphere. Yea, think about what the crooked or misguided politicians or other power hunger lowlifes could do if they learned to control these abilities. No, he would keep the secret between him, and a few close friends that needed to know. The carbon credits are not worth giving up humanities future.

After Stone paid Joe for the breakfast, he dropped half off for Buck and then went to the *Spiritus*. He walked over to the helm and switched on the deck lights. The inside of the cave lit up from the glow of the mast and spreader lights. He walked around the deck for a few minutes sipping his coffee. He then walked down into the cabin and looked around. It had been a few days and the inside had dried out nicely. There was still, nonetheless, the residual pungent smell of diesel mixed with bilge water, oil, and a sundry of other items. No matter what, it was still the *Spiritus* and she was ready to get back into the action after a few structural and cosmetic repairs. No matter Stone's ability to shift matter from one phase to another; or his ability to travel through time and space within the span of an eye's blink, he would always look to the *Spiritus* for a slow easy dependable ride to nowhere. It is there she whispers to him stories and inspirations gathered throughout the ages.

Stone went outside and released the lines from the shore before starting the engine. Even though the generator had been running for a couple of days, the *Spiritus* stored over a thousand gallons of diesel. There was plenty of fuel left over. He was behind the wheel when he thought about the calm waters of the Eau Gallie River in Melbourne, Florida.

The *Spiritus* was once again at her home base. Stone put the boat in gear and slowly moved forward towards Eau Gallie Boat Works. It was early morning before sunrise. Stone maneuvered the *Spiritus* into the railway docks and cut the engines. He left a note on the helm for Ed.

> *"The work is obvious. Have fun and call me when done. Still have a date with a Platypus when you are finished. Until then I need a rest."*
> STONE

Ed was a fourth generation sailor and a master shipwright. His great grandfather and grandfather were Naval Admirals. One of them became governor of Bermuda sometime in the eighteen hundreds.

His father and brother were also master craftsmen able to build boats from the keel up. Their family tradition was for the males to build urns in the form of a sailboat, into which their ashes after cremation would rest. Then while the sun is setting, surviving family members launch the boat in a special area along the western coastline. As the boat, sails out to sea it is set on fire and the ashes would eventually be committed to the sea. In these modern times, it was as close to a Viking Funeral anyone could legally find.

Edward owned and operated the 150-year-old yacht basin built on land deeded over to a private, by Abraham Lincoln, after the civil war: Stone knew the *Spiritus* was in caring professional hands.

Stone also had some historical business to take care that involved Alfredo's past; and then there was the immediate issues of Janet's lack of cancer, and Buck's itch to get married to a beautiful, confusingly feminine, but brilliant scientist.

For the moment, however, Stone was going to track down Janet and hold on to her for a few hours.

"Hello Janet"

Stone used his key to open the door for her apartment. Janet was sitting on the couch with a cup of coffee.

"Hello Stone…it is a miracle. One minute I had a malignant tumor, the next minute it is gone."

"Miracles happen, sort of, but regardless of that your doctor got it wrong. The tumor was not malignant."

"How do you know? Where did the lump go? The doctor took another x-ray this morning and it was completely gone. How can that be?"

"Janet, sometimes you simply have to accept things for what they are and move on. Maybe it was the herbal paste but more than likely not."

"Stone what is going on? Did you do something?"

"Yes."

"What? What did you do?"

"I fell in love with you and have never stopped. Will you come to bed with me?"

"What did you have in mind?"

"Perhaps, you and I could generate a lot of heat. Turn down the air before you come in. I'm going to take a shower first."

"Do you want some wine first?"

"It's kind of early but--sure."

In her best Jewish princess nasal tone she said, "I want to take a shower...too!"

"Funny girl, take your clothing off."

"That's your job, get to it bad-boy."

For years in the late evenings, after the restaurant closed, Stone and Alfredo would sit at a table and sip homemade limoncello; sometimes there were recipes made with tangerine, orange, and sometimes mint. Both Alfredo and Stone preferred the tangerine. Tonight was no different, except for the fact that Alfredo knew that Stone was somehow instrumental in saving his father from death at the hands of the Sicilian mafia.

"Sassolino, I have no words to say thank you. And I know you do not look for these words, but from my heart thank you." Alfredo began to cry. These were not tears from the moment; perhaps they were from memories of helplessness caused by events that happened many years before. Stone knew Alfredo's past and was gripped by the injustice. Stone loathed bullies.

It was during evenings like this when Alfredo would open up about New York. He never completely got over the frightening brutality and senseless cruelty rained down on him by the soldiers that called themselves Mafioso. Those bastards had no honor as they claimed to have; they were merely pigs and lowlife thieves. The real men of honor were the Beati Paoli from which the mafia deluded themselves into believing they were like. However, they only mocked the traditions of heroes through mimicry. The Beati Paoli were indeed true angels: warriors willing to die to recover another person's honor; Robin hoods that would steal back from the rich those items stolen from the poor; and then return the spoils back to the poor.

For whatever the reasons the Cosa Nostra and other crime organizations evolved into what they are today; or for whatever perverted reasons they continue to frame and justify their actions; Stone's friend continued to hurt deep in his soul from the events of that morning in New York City; and the shame he has had to internalize for many years.

It is never the event or the crime that scars a person; it is the helplessness resulting from the abuse of power. In retrospect, a person always feel they should have fought back, perhaps even die if that was what it would have taken, to preserve their honor. That may have preserved Alfredo's pride, but then in Alfredo's case, he would not have been in this future place. A place where he was needed, to make friends with a person that had the power to not only save his father from a kidnapping by the mafia; but also rid an entire Sicilian community of the scum that robbed a community daily of their liberty, justice, and freedoms.

Like an unseen butterfly that flaps its wings to start a hurricane, it was Alfredo having to suffer alone in silence, so that in the future many more would reap the benefits of his secret pain. Now Stone had the ability to edit out some of that historical pain without altering the future—too badly.

As Stone cautiously experimented with this new ability to 'edit' events, he found time to be an interesting concept. Except for a short few milliseconds into the future, there was simply no future time. Editing of film just does not happen until someone shoots the frames. There are no future events until they happen: future events are merely plans.

Researchers have found, however, the ability of the human brain to react to events before they happen--but that is all. In one supervised experiment, electrodes monitored a blind folded person's brainwaves. They show before a pinprick, or even before a needle is inserted into a vein, the brain prepares the body for the pain that it foresees. Even if a person is oblivious to anything that will be happening, the body is not: the body is a transmitter of data;

it also interprets incoming data. This is all the evidence science has to support any type of a future beyond a few milliseconds from the present. Reality evolves when photons bounce off matter and records that information within the history books of the evolutionary library and not before. There may be no future, but there certainly is a past.

There is no question, whatsoever, that a record of a past-history exists. Nathaniel Hawthorne once wrote, "Time flies over us, but leaves its shadow behind. Steven H. Lumbert wrote, "...the movie has been filmed and the lessons stored by the Librarian in every cosmic movie theater that exists. Each story is stored within every atom that forms every compound that comprises every molecule that makes up every cell that forms the structure of every living thing. The stories of failed experiments, as well the successful ones: the hurt, the joy, the wars won, and the battles lost. Not even a whisper is lost to the wind."

Stone figured out what the red and blue tints in the white energy of frozen time represented. It was like a person standing on the side of a railroad track with a speeding train coming at them. The sound of the train eventually gets louder and louder as it gets closer. These are the wavelengths of the sound getting smaller or shifting from blue within the electromagnetic spectrum. But as the train passes the sounds decrease and that means the wavelengths are getting longer or shifting to red within the electromagnetic spectrum: that is also called the Doppler Effect.

Another way to look at that concept is by holding a slinky fully stretched out by someone at the other end. As that person moves towards you, the coils (wavelengths) get closer and closer together--that is the blue shift: or in other words, you are looking at time in the past. As the person walks past you, the coils (wavelengths) once again start to expand as new history evolves, and time expands--that is the red shift.

An observers position along that slinky is their position in time. If they can barely see any red but here is a lot of blue then they are in the present. Moving towards the red moves the observer towards the future. If there is a lot of deep blue on one side and deep red on another, the observer is in the middle of history...somewhere.

Time is as a movie made of tiny little picture frames of action that normally move by too quickly to distinguish the individual frames. However, if an observer could freeze time, then each individual frame is susceptible to editing and study. That is what Stone is able to do, think about one particular picture frame in time and phase walk to that individual frame to edit the picture. Nevertheless, he has to be very careful.

Evolution happens because everyone and everything learns from what it does. Those lessons, every one of them are stored and are accessible to anyone who is astute enough to access them. The memory of those lessons help to build a higher level of complexity, and that allows species to adapt quickly, and to change in order to survive unexpected or catastrophic alterations to their environment.

Even atoms and their elemental particles had to go through an evolutionary process. They had to learn how to store those lessons in a type of memory and then create a method to pass those lessons upwards so higher levels of complexity could build.

This was how Stone was able to form the mental pictures he needed to enable his phase walks through time.

Stone knocked on the door of the still unopened New York Pizzeria. Alfredo came to the front door. "May I help you?"

"Excuse me Sir, I am very early for a meeting across the street, and I was hoping you would allow me to make some notes at your table. I would be more than glad to buy something or even rent the space for an hour."

"Sure, sure you-a come in sit anywhere you like. Can I get you some coffee; or a beer perhaps?"

"Espresso would be nice."

"Coming up," replied Alfredo.

Alfredo walked to the back room to get a fresh can of coffee to make the espresso. There waiting for him were three goons who broke-in from the back alley entrance. One hit him in the stomach, knocking the wind out of him. The other used a small bat to hit him on the back.

Alfredo fell to the floor and leaned against the wall. Vinnie yelled out, "You haven't paid us for three weeks now you shit!"

Stone walked up smiling towards the goons that were beating up a person, which in the future would become a very good friend.

Vinnie looked up surprised. That look soon turned to anger; he did not like to be disturbed while working. "What the hell do you want?"

"Just like to watch a "capra amante malato" screw around with someone that can't defend himself. You might as well beat up a crippled old woman you "sick goat lover." I bet you even prefer the little boy goats don't you. They don't kick as hard. You like everything easy don't you Vinnie."

"Hey how you know my name? Talking to me that way will get you killed."

"No it won't, I kick too much. That would be too scary for you."

"Bobbie shoot that idiot, I don't have time for this crap."

Bobbie and Marco both pulled their guns and pointed them at Stone. Alfredo was coughing and trying to catch his breath but still tried to tell the Stranger to go away, everything will be fine. The Stranger looked at Alfredo and smiled with confidence.

"Bobbie," Stone said aloud, "Would you please shoot Marco in the left knee cap." Stone wanted Vinnie to hear him loud and clear and understand there was a force in the world must larger than him. Vinnie could only stare at Bobbie with his mouth hanging open.

With a blank look on his face, Bobbie pointed his pistol at Marco's left knee and shot the kneecap off. Marco dropped to the ground but not before giving Vinnie, a gut shot by accident. Both were screaming and cussing at each other. Alfredo had covered his head in an attempt to deflect any ricochets.

"Bobbie, please shoot your own right knee cap off… please."

Bobbie aimed his weapon at his own right kneecap and then blew it off. With that, Bobbie quickly came out of his trance and joined the choir of other screamers.

Stone walked over and helped Alfredo get to his feet. He led him to a barstool. "My friend, are you ok?"

"Si, I am fine. Did you see that? They just shot each other. That was madness!"

"You can never really know what some people are thinking," replied Stone.

Stone picked up the phone and called for the police and then the ambulance. He then turned to Alfredo, please tell the police that the three goons came in to steal from you and they just began to shoot each other. I was never here if that is ok with you.

"My privilege sir."

"Alfredo, I need you to do one more thing, this is very important. Learn about Merritt Island, Florida there is lots of sunshine, cheap rent and most of all no mafia. We will meet again one day. Remember if you can these words 'What other dungeon is so dark as one's own heart! What Jailer so inexorable as one's self.'"

Most men cannot be angels and bastards at the same time. Nor should they be, there are men thrown into those roles by destiny so others do not have to endure that burden. It was so for the monks and priests of the Beati Paoli, it has been for Stone, and so it will always be for innocent by-standers, the lovers of life, like Alfredo.

Stone then walked over to the screaming goon choir. He towered over them and waited until all their eyes were on him. In their minds he became il Diavolo with glowing red eyes, they were in hell with fire blazing all around them. He reached down and removed all their hands. "Do you know where you are and who I am?"

The swine were screaming even louder as they looked at the stubs where their hands use to be. "Who are you, what do you want?"

"I have an offer you would be stupid to refuse."

When the police got there, nothing made sense. How could people without hands shoot each other and beat up an innocent restaurant owner. There must have been another person that shot the goons and left guns behind to confuse the crime scene.

There was something else very curious about this crime, every one of the goons are crying out, not only their involvement in this crime, but also many, many more. They wanted to confess and make restitution. The investigators just looked at each other as they continued to make notes and recordings of the confessions; that is, after the criminals were read their Miranda warning.

Again, Stone and Alfredo were laughing and celebrating Roberto's rescue from the mafia: more so, the fact that the most ruthless Don's, their capos, and their soldiers had confessed their crimes and returned all the proceeds from their crimes.

The community pooled the money and used it to purchase farm equipment so they could collectively farm and work the new lands the community now owns.

Alfredo looked at Stone hard, with a question forming on his face, he asked, "What other dungeon is so dark as one's own heart! What Jailer so inexorable as one's self?"

Stone said, "Nathanial Hawthorne, nice. So Alfredo do you have darkness in your heart, regrets for things you should have done?"

"Like anyone, a few, but nothing I cannot live with. Let me ask you a question, did you ever eat at a pizzeria in New York about 20 years ago."

"I love New York," Stone replied.

Many things may have been altered in the future, because of Stone's interference in the past. But Stone was not sorry his friend was never robbed of his self-respect.

A few days later Buck invited all his friends to a dinner party he asked Alfredo to prepare. A special guest was invited from Stone's past that offered to do Buck a favor.

Stone use to have an oversized house on the Indian River Lagoon: on Saturday mornings around 2am, after 10 or 15 black label scotch-whiskeys loaded with bitters, Father Nick would find his way to the couch on the back porch so he could wake up looking over the Indian River. The back door was always open for friends. When he woke, Stone would typically make breakfast. More than once, they would spend the entire morning fishing on the dock while pontificating on the ideas of God and religion. Even then, Stone had no use for religion, but could not resist trying to understand more about its origins.

Nick would reciprocate and allow Stone to sleep at a Benedictine Monastery when he visited him in West Palm Beach. That is until one morning two half-dressed girls walked out of Stone's room and asked some of the other flabbergasted Priests, where the coffee was.

Stone explained that in the wee morning hours, Nikos Kazantzakis spoke to him from these walls. He spoke about happiness: a glass of wine, a roasted chestnut, the sound of the sea, the sound of a woman's undergarments hitting the stone floors. It was his duty as a vessel of God, to explore the external expression of an inward cry that seeks answers to the most profound questions of existence being sought behind these walls. Besides the thrill of "bumping uglies" in a monastery was simply too hard for a girl to pass up.

The other priests did not like the explanation at all, but Nick understood what was going on. Taboos were made to abuse. The limits of a person's independence and individuality must always be tested. Sacred cows that strangle innovation must be slaughtered. When taboos are broken they release fire into an independent's blood and causes him to break away the chains that bind, setting himself free, and all those that dare to follow. That is how humanity slowly climbs out of mediocrity, away from their comfortable cocoons—to find new air to breath. It is how youth fights for sunshine kept away by overshadowing elders.

Kazantzakis and Stone were kindred spirits in virtually all matters: Both of them looked to nature for answers about God and life. Nikos Kazantzakis was famous for walking up to an almond tree asking it to speak to him about God, and with that, the tree bloomed. Stone use to listen to the stories trees had to tell, now he sees them as he sees all things, brothers and sisters all born from the same bowl of energy; everything destined to return to that same bowl; our only difference being, the contributions we make to life while in the solid phase.

Attending the feast was Father Nick, Barbara, Alfredo, Linda, Bob and Dr. Rick, Stone and Janet: then there was Buck and most of his old SEAL team all in full formal military dress. Also attending was

Buck's old commander who was now the President's National Security Advisor. Buck called this the retirement party he never had.

After cocktails and some appetizers, the National Security Advisor stood up and began to make a toast.

"Throughout the ages men and women have sacrificed their lives and livelihoods to make this world a better place for others to live. The life that Buck has lived, on behalf of the American people, will never be read about in history books. His unsung accomplishments locked away in files, never revealed.

"It is with great trepidation, but also elation that I formally offer you into civilian life a man whose honor has no boundaries. Buck the President has asked me to offer you his most profound thank you for your service to the country.

"Now, Nick, Barbara, and Buck will you please come forward and stand with me."

They got up and moved to the front of the room. The new commander of the SEAL team called his men to attention. They stood up straight as he also commanded, "Forward March!"

The Soldiers formed two straight lines, one by Barbara the other by Buck, "Present Arms!" Their swords went sharply into the air and crossed forming an arch for the others to see through.

Buck removed the sword from his belt, still in the scabbard, he handed it to his ex-commander.

The National Security Advisor started once more, "In the days of old, when a warrior was fortunate enough to retire from the battle field, he would return home and give his wife the sword he carried as a symbol of his retirement from battle, and his willingness to build a new and peaceful life with her.

"If he did not have a wife he would wait until he found the women that brought joy back into his life."

The ex-commander returned the sword back to Buck.

Buck turned towards Barbara and kneeled in front of her holding out his sword for her to take: my sword to always protect you, my heart is yours to do, as you will; my arms to work for your happiness. I don't need promises or vows from you, I only want to know that you want to enjoy life with me."

Barbara, with tears running down her cheeks could not speak. Nick leaned in towards her, "this is when a girl who likes a gent and wants to marry him says yes or no; either way the food is getting cold and ice is melting into my black label scotch."

Only one word came from her lips, she could not speak any more.

Everyone stood up and clapped. Barbara had a death grip around Buck's neck. Buck looked at Barbara, "If you want a formal ceremony we can have one. Right now this is all I need."

"This is perfect Buck. How much more perfect could it get?"

The ex-commander said, "Leave it to a SEAL to pull off a surprise attack."

The entire SEAL unit exclaimed, "Hoo-yah!

Buck put a ring on Barbara's finger, gave her a long kiss, and then pulled out a signed marriage license and gave it to her, "All it needs is your signature and Nicks. I am pretty sure Stone and Janet will also sign as witnesses."

"How did you do this without me?"

The National Security Advisor broke in, "He had a little help from some friends that wanted him off the market. That way they would have a chance with the other pretty girls once more."

Buck spoke up, "Let's eat; the food and drinks are on me!"

Alfredo interrupted, "No way, we don't serve cheap beer here; so everything is on the house as gratitude for Buck's help in saving my father from the mafia low-life animals in Sicily."

Barbara looked at Buck, "When did you do that?"

"That's another one of those stories, I can't tell you everything about. You wouldn't believe most of it anyway," replied Buck.

"That has got to stop."

"Si, il mio amore."

Edward and his wife Kendal walked in the front door late for the ceremony, but just in time for the banquet. Ed walked over to Stone and handed him a gift.

"Ed the party is for Buck?" said Stone.

Edward replied, "Just thought you would like that in your hands, as soon as possible."

Stone opened the box: a custom key for the Spiritus was in it. Stone looked at this master Boatwright and poured him a Scotch. On the key was inscribed, "Inspiration is never lost to the wind."

Janet reached over and took Stone's hand, "So where is your sword Tiger?"

"Only a SEAL swings it around in public, my lady; a gentleman finds a more private cozy place before it leaves the scabbard."

"I don't know; I kind of liked the whole surprise, sword brandishing thing."

"Stone can I have a private word with you; I am sorry to intrude but I have to leave early and I won't have another chance." The National Security Advisor was standing next to Stone and Janet.

Janet looked at Stone with one eyebrow cocked up, "Go, but you are not getting out of it that easily."

"Sir, your timing is impeccable. That conversation was headed for dangerous waters."

"You don't reach executive levels at the White House without being observant."

The subject of the Democratic Republic of the Congo was put on the table and how farm cooperatives like the 9 Tomatoes a Day program might be able to help. It was a discussion requiring immediate attention. Stone would be attending more meetings very soon.

A few weeks later after the excitement had calmed down, Stone returned to his routine of going to Alfredo's for lunch and an afternoon espresso. One day when he arrived, Alfredo was flustered again. "What's up my friend?"

"Sometime it-a like New York all over again! This person and that one, coming in-a, extorting money for this little thing or that."

"What happened now?"

"There is an inspector writing tickets right now in the kitchen because he found a dead bug behind a cabinet next to the door. I have been frying food all morning and grease is on the back splash. He says the kitchen is not clean. That is crazy. My kitchen is cleaned every night: everywhere! I cannot help if a bug comes in when the door opens. At least it dies when it come-a in."

"Can't do anything about that Alfredo."

"I know; I know Sassolino, thanks for listening. Have a Peroni, it will break your legs, I promise."

The Inspector wrote his tickets and went out the back door to his car. When he got in, Stone was standing nearby.

The Inspector tried starting the engine of his private car; it backfired and then would not start. The Inspector opened the hood and saw smoke was coming out of the engine. As he searched for the origins of the fire, the hood came crashing down hitting the back of his head. The Inspector fell backwards to the ground.

The Inspector could hear himself think. "Shitty behavior begets shitty behavior. There was no need to be that rough with Alfredo. His kitchen is always clean. The man was working you twerp; of course, there will be grease on the back splash. The Universe may not always reward good behavior but it will certainly rain down trouble for the bad you do. So fix it."

The Inspector stood up and closed the hood of the car. He walked over and knocked, once again, on the back door of Alfredo's Restaurant. When Alfredo opened it the Inspector said, "Alfredo, we need to talk."

"Please come in."

"I'm sorry; I was thinking I may have been too rough on the inspection. You always have a clean restaurant. Please return the tickets to me."

Alfredo gladly did what the Inspector asked.

"Ok, get rid of the bug Alfredo and this never happened. I am sorry, we are all trying to make a living; a hard working person like you, does not need this kind of grief in his life. We are all in this game together. Again, I am sorry."

Afterward, the Inspector turned and walked out the door. Alfredo saw the smoke coming out to the car's hood.

"Everything is ok?"

"Don't know; I am calling the tow service."

"Please come in and wait at the bar. I will make you a sandwich and drink." The Inspector sat down at the bar next to Stone.

Stone said, "It's amazing how much better a day becomes when we stop making other people's lives miserable isn't it. All we have to do is re-calibrate our thinking about what makes our jobs important."

"Sorry Sir, do I know you?"

"Not really, it's become a habit lately; I get into people's heads now and then; just to help remind them why we walk the Earth. Here have a Peroni; it will break your legs."

THE END OF BOOK ONE:
PHASE WALKING SERIES

To learn more about *I Beati Paoli* go to the website www.thebeatipaoliandthedevilshand.com or visit the publisher's website www.abspublishers.com to find more books written by Charles S. Darwin III.

Once again, in the second book of the Phase Walking Series, Stone Richards and Buck go against rebel armies; but this time, those being injured have also turned against the wrong doers. Buck helps to train the new warriors at the request of the American President and the Secretary of State; Stone stands close by, always watching with his quantum abilities at the ready if necessary. The Congo Conspiracy demonstrates that a nation rebuilds itself from the bottom up and with the blood of its own people, not with the help from corporations intend on making profit from those that control the mineral wealth.

www.ingramcontent.com/pod-product-compliance
Lightning Source LLC
Chambersburg PA
CBHW070507260626
47161CB00004B/1485